KISS ME, CREEP

"What is it with you two?" Leona asked me in the locker room. "I've never seen a guy get to you the way Richie does."

"It's simple," I said. "We can't stand each other."

"I think he's cute," she said. "And I know a lot of girls who would kill for a chance to go out with him."

"He could be the cutest guy in the world, and I still wouldn't go out with him," I assured her. "And I'm sure the feeling is mutual. We can't even look at each other without getting into an argument."

"It sounds romantic." Leona sighed.

"About as romantic as a date with Godzilla," I answered, trying hard not to think about Richie's beautiful blue eyes.

Bantam Sweet Dreams Romances
Ask your bookseller for the books you have missed

Kiss Me, Creep

Marian Woodruff

BANTAM BOOKS
TORONTO • NEW YORK • LONDON • SYDNEY • AUCKLAND

RL 6, IL age 11 and up

KISS ME, CREEP
A Bantam Book / June 1984

*Sweet Dreams and its associated logo are registered trademarks of
Bantam Books, Inc. Registered in U.S. Patent and Trademark Office
and elsewhere.*

Cover photo by Pat Hill

ISBN 0-553-24150-8

Published simultaneously in the United States and Canada

*Bantam Books are published by Bantam Books, Inc. Its trademark,
consisting of the words "Bantam Books" and the portrayal of a
rooster, is Registered in U.S. Patent and Trademark Office and in
other countries. Marca Registrada. Bantam Books, Inc., 666 Fifth
Avenue, New York, New York 10103.*

PRINTED IN THE UNITED STATES OF AMERICA

O   0 9 8 7

To Mary and Michael

Chapter One

When Richie Brennan and I met each other that day long ago, it was hate at first sight. I've heard about this thing called chemistry—though so far it's never happened to me—where two people look at each other and—zap! They're in love. Is it possible, I wonder, that there's such a thing as *reverse* chemistry? A girl and a boy meet; they gaze into each other's eyes; and—presto! They can't stand each other. That's the way it was with us. The classic mismatch. Oil and vinegar. Fire and water. Rainy days and picnics. Richie Brennan and yours truly, Joy Wilder. From the very beginning we were destined to bump heads.

Our first fateful meeting took place during my sophomore year. That was the year my mom, my brother, and I moved from Seattle to Piper's

Point. Coming into a new school was scary. I'd never had any trouble making friends at my old school, but I couldn't help thinking how hard it would be in a small town where all the kids had probably known one another since kindergarten. Also, I didn't know what to wear here. Back at Columbus High in Seattle, jeans and T-shirts had practically been mandatory uniforms, but I worried that maybe kids dressed up more here. So for my first day of school I settled on something in-betweenish—my denim prairie skirt and a puffy-sleeved cotton blouse. There was a tiny mustard stain on one of the sleeves, but I didn't think anybody would notice it. Besides, I kind of liked that stain. It had nostalgic meaning for me. I'd gotten it when I was trying to eat a hot dog while simultaneously crying my eyes out.

On that morning of my first day of school in Piper's Point, I inspected myself critically in the mirror. I imagined I was a stranger, seeing the person before me for the first time. Did she look like someone I might want to get to know? Maybe. I decided I didn't look too bad. Actually, I realized, I looked pretty good. But my external appearance was the best part of me that morning. Inside I felt like a mess.

Disaster struck when I was on my way to school. Halfway there, our old Pontiac station wagon got a flat tire. Between the two of us, Mom and me, it took half an hour to change it. By the time I got to school, I was ready to turn around and go home again. My hair was a mess; my shoes were caked with mud; and the big streak of mud down the front of my skirt would not come off, no matter how many wet paper towels I scrubbed it with in the girls' bathroom. All I got for my efforts was a big wet spot over the mud. To top everything off, I was nearly forty minutes late.

After several wrong turns, I found the school office and was in the midst of having my schedule typed up when a boy walked in. He was tall, with a mass of dark, curly hair, and he had incredible light blue eyes. I could tell immediately, by the way he was whistling to himself and sort of strolling around with his hands stuffed in his front pockets, that he was very popular. Casually he asked the secretary for a late slip, as if being late for class were the last thing on his mind.

While waiting for the secretary to get to his note, he glanced over her shoulder at what she was typing for me. Then he looked at me.

3

"New, huh?"

I looked at him out of the corner of my eye. I couldn't tell if he was really staring at me that hard, or if I was just imagining it, but I wasn't about to look at him directly. Realizing how messy I looked, I squirmed with embarrassment and hoped that he was nearsighted and couldn't see me clearly. I decided to pretend I hadn't known he was talking to me. There were a few other people milling around the office, so it wasn't a hundred percent unlikely that he was addressing somebody else. But he wasn't the type to give up easily.

"I said, are you new?" he asked in a slightly louder voice, as if I might be hard of hearing.

I nodded quickly. "Uh-huh." Now that I'd answered his question, maybe we could drop the subject.

No such luck. He peered over the secretary's shoulder again. Out loud, he read, "Wilder, Joy." Then he turned to me with a grin that was almost a smirk and repeated, "Wilder Joy. Hey, I like it. Sounds adventurous. But I guess most people must call you Joy Wilder. That's OK, but a lot less exciting. I think I'll just call you J.W."

The grin had spread from the corners of his mouth up to his light blue eyes. Was he making fun of me? Since first grade, boys had been making fun of my name. There was this guy at my old school who used to go around telling a really dumb riddle about me. It went like this:

Q. What do you call a date with Joy Wilder?
A. A wild joy ride.

Pretty stupid, right? I thought so, but it made plenty of people laugh, and I guess it made me sort of sensitive about my name. It also made me think—for a long time—that boys just didn't like me that much. But then I realized that maybe that's just the way certain boys are. I've noticed that a lot of the time the ones who tease you the most are the ones who would like to ask you out but are afraid. Then, after they've been teasing you awhile, they're afraid that if they ever tried acting serious, you'd laugh.

So here was this strange boy making fun of my name on my very first day of school. Needless to say, I was not enchanted, even though I couldn't help noticing how good-looking he was.

"Cute," I mumbled disgustedly.

His grin took off into a full-fledged laugh. "Yeah, I've always thought so."

5

I stared at him. "Are you always this conceited?"

"Only when I'm trying to make a good impression. I'm normally the shy and humble type."

"I'll bet."

"By the way," he said, sticking out his hand, "I'm Richie Brennan."

I shook it unenthusiastically. "Hi."

"Hey, you're not nervous, are you?"

"How could I possibly be nervous?"

"I know this is your first day here and all, but, listen, we're not such a bad bunch. Don't go by me. Most of the inmates here aren't too dangerous."

"That's reassuring to know."

He was staring at the front of my skirt. "Hey, what happened? Looks like you ran into something."

I could feel myself starting to blush. "It was a flat tire."

"You changed it yourself?" That smirk again.

"What's so funny about that?"

"Nothing. It's just—well, you just don't look like the type who goes around changing tires, that's all."

That really got me. I mean, what did this creep know about me, anyway? Just because he happened to be a tall, dark, handsome creep didn't give him the right to go around judging people at first glance. I knew he wasn't being very serious; he was only making fun of me, but for some reason I felt like crying. Everything about my first day at Cabrillo High seemed to be going wrong. However, I wasn't about to let Richie Brennan know how I was feeling.

"Actually, I won the gold medal for changing tires in the last Olympics," I tossed back coolly.

"Ah, and a sense of humor besides!" Richie put a hand over his heart and rolled his eyes toward the ceiling. "I think I'm in love!"

I could see right through this guy's game. Right at that very moment there were probably fifty girls at Cabrillo High who had crushes on him. He probably thought all he had to do was switch on the charm machine to make the new girl number fifty-one. Me, the mud-covered stranger who didn't know a soul in town, and him, the handsome, popular superstar with hordes of women at his feet. I was sure that if you had asked Richie Brennan my name ten minutes after he'd met me, he wouldn't remember it. He was just playing with me—the way a cat plays with a mouse.

I fixed my gaze on the yellow registration card

that was slowly rolling its way up through the secretary's typewriter. What was taking so long? I willed her to hurry up. Finally she handed the card to me, stopping only long enough to scrawl her signature on a late slip for Richie first. By the time I turned around, he was disappearing through the doorway.

"See you around, J.W.!" he called and waved.

My first class was biology. I found the room without too much trouble. The hard part was trying to sneak in so that no one would notice me. The period was almost over, so I figured I could give my card to the teacher afterward. I opened the door a crack and slipped in sideways, crab-style. Luckily there was an empty chair in the back of the room. I was in the midst of sinking into it when a loud voice caused me to freeze.

There I was, sort of crouched over in midair, half in and half out of my seat, when this person next to me started to yell, "Hey, it's J.W.! Talk about fate. I didn't expect to see *you* again so soon!"

Suddenly everybody in the whole class was staring at me. Thirty pairs of eyes fixed on me with the kind of deadly fascination you usually see in a biology class when the teacher passes around a bottled shark's brain or a jar of baby tarantulas.

Not that I'm a freak or anything. I'm very normal looking. My hair is the color of nutmeg—a cross between brown and browner, with a little red thrown in for good measure. It's short and naturally curly, which people with straight hair sometimes envy—but only because they don't know what it's like to have it frizz up in damp weather. My eyes are greenish-gray and sort of tipped up at the corners. I think my mouth is too big—in more ways than one—but maybe it's my imagination since no one's ever said anything about it.

Right then, though, I couldn't have felt more freakish than if I'd suddenly sprouted two extra heads. And all thanks to Richie Brennan, who was sitting right next to me. How had I managed to get so lucky twice in a row? Little did I know that this was just the beginning.

All through my sophomore year and into my junior year, Richie continued to plague me. Mostly with little things—like after weeks of ignoring me, he'd turn around suddenly and say something outrageous, like, "Hey, J.W., if you're not too busy this weekend, how about eloping to

Reno?" He got a big kick out of watching me turn red.

The J.W. part really got to me, too. Nobody else ever called me by my initials. It was strictly Richie's thing, which made it seem as if there was something going on between us—and there most definitely was not.

During my junior year, when I got on the cheerleading squad, I'd see him sitting in the front row of the bleachers during football games, shooting me his cocky grin and waiting for me to slip up. And the harder I tried to ignore him, the more mistakes I'd make and the more Richie seemed to enjoy himself.

This year, my senior year, Richie and I were in the same social studies class. Everything was going along fine—which meant that I'd managed to ignore Richie pretty successfully—until Mr. Jaeger chose us as opponents in one of the class's debating sessions. I groaned when I saw what the subject of our debate was going to be. Mr. Jaeger had written on the blackboard: THE EQUAL RIGHTS AMENDMENT: SHOULD IT PASS? I was to be on the pro side, Richie on the con. Naturally. That wouldn't be hard for him—Richie was the biggest male chauvinist around. When I looked over at him, he winked at me as though the whole thing were a huge joke.

I should have known I was in for it, but on the day of our debate, he still managed to take me by surprise. I had arrived fully armed with my index cards arranged in perfect order. I had done a lot of homework, and I was prepared to present the best, most reasonable arguments possible in favor of passing the ERA. But then Richie walked in wearing a frilly pink apron, and all attempts at seriousness flew right out the window. He'd stolen the show. It was at least five minutes before everyone stopped laughing and we could get down to business. But even so, nothing went right after that entrance. All Richie had to do was arch an eyebrow or purse his lips in a certain way, and the class was off again, laughing hysterically.

I went up to him when the period was over. "I'll bet you really do think boys are smarter, don't you?"

"Come on, J.W. I was only kidding around. It was supposed to be a joke."

"Well, in case you haven't noticed, I'm not laughing."

"It wouldn't hurt you to crack a smile once in a

while, you know," he said. "You could be really pretty if you tried."

That did it. I saw red. "What makes you so sure I'm interested in whether or not you think I'm pretty? Richie Brennan, you are the most stuck-up, conceited creep in this entire school!"

I was hoping that that would get him, but he just shrugged and laughed.

Then he did something really, unbelievably awful. The worst thing he had ever done to me up until then. Worse than if he'd hauled off and hit me.

Richie kissed me.

Right in front of everyone, he leaned over and touched his lips to mine. I could feel them sort of twitching, as if he were trying not to laugh. Otherwise, they were dry and warm.

The most incredible part was that I just stood there. I was so stunned I couldn't move. I watched him stroll off, whistling some obscure tune as though nothing whatsoever had happened. It was one of those situations where you can't think of anything to say at that moment, but half an hour later you think of half a million put-downs.

On Richie, I would've liked to use them all.

Chapter Two

"One—two—three—KICK!"

I jumped up, kicked my legs out in a midair split, and landed neatly in a squatting position with my weight on my toes. A neat trick that I'm sure wouldn't have qualified me for Ringling Brothers, but it was ambitious enough for the head cheerleader of a high school nobody had ever heard of. Leona, Beth, and Torey tried it, then collapsed onto a stack of mats with a chorus of groans and mutinous mutterings.

"I love you, Joy," said Leona Bennett, rubbing at a sore muscle in her thigh, "but my legs hate you. I'm not exactly Jo-Jo Starbuck, you know. You could try taking it a little easier with us once in a while."

"Joy doesn't know the meaning of taking it easy," Beth Orlando said, groaning dramatically and tossing her long, silky black hair over one shoulder.

True, taking it easy wasn't exactly my style. According to my grandfather, Hank Wilder, I'm the proverbial cyclone on wheels. I don't know about that, but once I could walk, they couldn't stop me. At a very early age, I learned how to climb out of my crib. At night my mother would raise the sides of the crib as high as they would go, but I would manage to get out. Those night rampages, as my mother describes them, were the stuff legends are made of. Unfortunately I don't remember any of that stuff. These days, my energy is channeled into more constructive activities than covering walls with lipstick graffiti.

"Is it my fault you're a bunch of lazy slobs?" I asked, teasing. "Come on, let's run through the routine one more time. We only have a few more minutes before the jocks take over, so let's hurry." I was referring to our beloved basketball team, of course.

Torey Sinclair moaned. "Listen to her. A walking Geritol commercial. OK, slave driver. Just remember, if I die during this practice it'll be your fault."

I giggled. "Don't worry. We'll tell everyone you died for the glory of your school."

We all found that one particularly hilarious, since none of us could imagine sacrificing ourselves for the sake of good old Cabrillo High. I mean, it's a great school and all, but certainly nothing to get choked up about.

Leona pushed her hair out of her eyes and gave an exasperated sigh as she scrambled to her feet. Beth and Torey followed suit, falling in behind me.

"First," I said, "you've got to close your eyes and imagine the band is playing. The crowd is going bananas. Parky Roberts just scored a touchdown in the last two seconds of the final quarter—"

"In which case, you're about to be trampled by the fans," a male voice boomed across the gym.

My eyes flew open. Richie—I should have known! I figured he was expecting me to do something dumb like turn red or start fidgeting with the zipper on my warm-ups, but I stood my ground, giving him a defiant look that would have turned Clint Eastwood's knees to jelly.

The trouble was, Richie didn't flinch. He stared right back. We were starting a real eyeball-to-eyeball showdown. A silent duel of wits. Having a younger brother at home, on whom I'd practiced quite a bit, I considered myself a master of this game. Unfortunately Richie was a master, too. We stared and stared, but the showdown between us ended when I looked away first. My only thought was that Richie must have had more than one brother or sister at home. This was a minor, but nevertheless significant, victory on his part.

"What do you want?" I asked. I had forgotten it was the basketball team's turn to use the gym.

He pointed at the big mesh-covered clock over the scoreboard. "Time's up, girls. The locker-room natives are getting restless."

"Mind if we finish up with this last routine?" I asked stiffly.

I was determined to hold my ground. My fellow cheerleaders didn't help matters, however. They broke out in a fresh chorus of groans. I turned around and shot them my best I'll-get-you-for-this glare. The groans turned into giggles. I guess I'm just not the menacing type.

"Be my guest," said Richie, with a grand sweep of his arm, "but better make it quick. I take no responsibility for any injuries that might occur in the event of a stampede."

"Thanks so much," I replied in my most sickeningly sweet voice.

Richie was acting as if he owned the whole gym and was doing us a gigantic favor by letting us use it. A wave of heat was spreading up my neck and onto my cheeks. Why did Richie always have this effect on me? Why couldn't I just ignore him, the way I ignored Henry Pflug, this nerdy guy in my English class who threw spitballs at the ceiling whenever the teacher's back was turned?

I felt Richie's eyes on me even after I turned my back. I've always hated books that say, "She felt his eyes boring into her." It sounds so dumb. I always imagined the guy coming up behind the girl with a pair of drills sprouting from his forehead like horns. But as corny as it sounds, that was how I really felt just then. I actually *felt* him staring at me.

The rest I'd just as soon forget. It happened during one of my high kicks. I must have kicked a little too high because all of a sudden the floor was sliding out from under me. I landed with a thud in the most ungraceful position possible— right smack on my behind.

"Oooohhh," I groaned, more from embarrassment than pain.

17

A large hand appeared in front of me. I took it without thinking.

"You OK?" Richie asked. His clasp was warm and very firm as he hauled me to my feet. My own skin felt hot and clammy next to his.

"Thanks," I muttered. "I'm all right."

He was still holding my hand, and for a second I could've almost sworn he was genuinely concerned about me. Then the mocking grin was back.

"If that's a preview, I can't wait to see the show," he said.

I yanked my hand away. He'd done it again. Once more he'd succeeded in making me feel like a complete idiot. How could one boy be so infuriating?

"Haven't you got anything better to do than hang around watching us practice?"

An innocent expression on his face, Richie turned to my friends. "See what I get for trying to help a damsel in distress? I'm telling you, it doesn't pay to be polite these days."

"Better watch who you pick up the next time," said Beth.

I put on my brightest, phoniest smile and took a deep breath. "I just hope I can return the favor someday," I said through gritted teeth.

"Now that," Richie said, "might even be worth the tumble."

See what I mean about Richie? He used so much energy being obnoxious to me that if he ever decided to quit doing it he'd probably have had to take up alligator wrestling as an alternative hobby.

"Catch you later, J.W.," he added, tossing it over his shoulder as he sauntered off in that casual I'm-in-no-hurry-to-get-there way of his.

I noticed with irritation that all three of my friends were following his exit with fascinated expressions. From what I had observed, Richie seemed to affect all girls that way.

All girls except me, of course.

Chapter Three

"What is it with you two?" Leona asked as we were taking a shower in the locker room. "I've never seen a guy get under your skin the way Richie does."

"It's simple," I said. "We can't stand each other."

"I think he's cute," said Torey.

"You think everybody's cute," cut in Beth. "I'll bet you'd even go out with Malcolm Pritchard if he asked."

Torey made a face. Malcolm is the president of the Computer Math Club; he's the kind of boy who wears his pants up to his armpits and under whose name in the yearbook is written: "My goal in life is to outdo Einstein." He's actually a pretty nice kid, but definitely out of it, if you know what I mean. Torey is boy crazy, but not *that* boy crazy.

"Richie and Malcolm aren't exactly in the same category," Leona protested. "Malcolm's from another planet."

Leona had her bushy blond hair lathered into a mound of shampoo suds. She molded it into an extravagant style, then strutted around the shower pretending to be one of the Coneheads from "Saturday Night Live." She's the real comic of our crowd. Most of the time all she has to do is look at us a certain way, and we break up into uncontrollable hysterics.

"Yeah," said Torey, "I know a lot of girls who would kill for the chance to go out with Richie. Don't you think he looks a little like Rick Springfield? Only maybe a little shorter."

Actually, now that she mentioned it, he did look a little like Rick, with that dark, curly hair and those light blue, laser-beam eyes, but I was bugged by the comparison. I didn't want to think of Richie the same way I did about Rick, whose poster hung over my bed at home.

"Short on personality, you mean," I muttered.

"You really don't like him, do you?" Beth peered at me through billows of steam.

"I *hate* him!"

21

"Mrs. Geller says that when a person says they hate someone it's really a kind of backward love," said Torey.

Mrs. Geller is our psychology teacher. She wears her gray hair in a ponytail and smokes these skinny black cigars. I think she has a secret crush on Sigmund Freud.

"You could turn Richie upside down, and I still wouldn't like him," I assured her. "And I'm sure the feeling is mutual. We can't even look at each other without getting into an argument."

Leona interrupted. "It sounds romantic. Like Spencer Tracy and Katharine Hepburn." Leona is a big fan of late-night TV. Her favorite show is "Dialing For Dollars Movie."

"The two of you are both too stubborn to admit you could probably like each other if you ever gave it a try," said Beth.

"Somebody has to start first," joined in Torey. "It might as well be you."

I made a loud, strangled noise. "Will you guys please let up? What is this—Down On Joy Day?"

"Don't be so sensitive," Leona said. "You know we love you just the way you are. If it wasn't for your stubbornness, we wouldn't have won first place in the cheerleading regionals. You never gave our aching muscles a break."

We'd gotten out of the shower and were toweling off.

"Speaking of competition," yelled Beth above the whir of Leona's hair dryer, "I hear the results of the senior poll are coming out in this week's paper."

The senior poll was one of the highlights of the semester. All the seniors had gotten a chance to vote for a boy and a girl in each of several categories. Malcolm Pritchard would probably get Most Likely to Succeed. Leona had a good shot at Best Sense of Humor, and Torey, with her flyaway strawberry blond hair and dreamy blue eyes, was a cinch for Prettiest.

"I'll bet Joy wins Cutest Smile," speculated Torey. "Who could resist those dimples?"

Did I forget to mention I have dimples? My brother, Kevin, says they make me look like I was kicked in the face by a donkey. Everyone else thinks they're adorable. I hate them. No one ever takes you seriously when you have dimples.

Leona looked up from rubbing lotion on her leg. "Unless they come up with a new category for Most Sadistic. Ouch! I'll be lucky if I can walk in the morning."

I was silent as I finished getting dressed. Actually, until that moment, I hadn't given the senior poll too much thought. Too many other things were filling my mind. Like the D+ I'd gotten on my history exam, for instance. Mrs. Ryan had penciled in a big red question mark next to the grade. I knew she was wondering what had happened to me since the beginning of the semester. My average had gone from about a B to a C-. She even tried to talk to me about it once—in a roundabout way. I could tell she suspected I was having trouble at home, but she just couldn't bring herself to come right out and ask. Mrs. Ryan is OK, but she's too polite to approach certain situations. She'd be way too delicate to ask, for instance, if my parents are getting a divorce or if a member of my family is dying of cancer. Suppose they were? She probably wouldn't want to talk about it anyway.

The truth wasn't so terrible when you compared it to those kinds of things, but it was a problem nevertheless. At least to me it was. An embarrassing problem. It concerned my mother and my soon-to-be-stepfather, Paul, who was twenty-eight years old. That made him only eleven years older than me—and exactly nine years younger than my mother. Personally, I happened to think it was pretty weird and upsetting, but the funny part was that I liked Paul.

Kevin and I called him Paul Bunyan because he's really enormous, about six foot six, with sandy blond hair and a bushy reddish beard. Everything else about him is big, too. He has this big booming laugh, and once he ate twenty-four pancakes in one sitting. I know because Kev and I counted.

So, Paul was not someone I could easily hate, even if I tried, which, believe me, I had. He was nice to Kev and me, too—even when Mom wasn't around, which proved he wasn't just faking it. Actually, I wouldn't have minded having Paul as an older brother, but whenever the subject of the wedding came up, I got sick.

No one knew I was about to have a stepfather who was practically the same age as I was. I tried talking to Mom about it, but she said I was more worried about what other people would think than what went on in our own family. Maybe she was right. I didn't know. I guessed nothing would really change since Paul practically lived with us then anyway. But it still worried me.

I guess a lot of things had always worried me, come to think of it. It's funny, though. If you're fairly pretty and somewhat popular and don't have too much trouble getting dates, then people think your life is practically perfect, and you have total self-confidence. Well, that's absolutely untrue. I don't think I'm all that pretty, for one thing. I'm OK, but like I said, I think maybe my mouth is too big, and I know for a fact my nose is on the stubby side. Then there was the matter of dates. I still worried about them. I worried about getting them when I didn't have them. And when I did have one, I worried about what to wear and say or whether that red blotch on my chin would turn into a zit by the time the guy came to pick me up.

I would sometimes worry about being too fat, which according to the weight-height chart tacked above the scale in the school nurse's office I wasn't. But whenever I thought my stomach was sticking out a little too far, I would get depressed and do something dumb like go home and eat an entire Sara Lee German chocolate cake. Sometimes I didn't even wait for it to thaw out. When you're head cheerleader, no one, except your very best friends, would ever suspect you of doing such gross things.

That's what I didn't like about Richie Brennan. His assumptions about people, I mean. He was one of those people who thought that if a girl was popular, she was automatically stuck-up. And if she was stuck-up, then she was just a big hot air balloon waiting to be deflated. Richie was always trying to deflate me, and a lot of the time he succeeded, only I wouldn't dream of ever letting him know it. It would only make him more conceited than he already was.

"Is Buddy taking you to the senior prom?" Leona asked me as we left the gym building and went hiking off to crafts class together.

I say "hiking" because Cabrillo High is built on the side of a hill overlooking the Juan de Fuca Strait, which is really beautiful, especially on a clear day when you can see all the little islands strung out like stars in an evergreen Milky Way.

I shrugged. "I guess so. He hasn't really asked. He just assumes I know he's going to."

I'd only been dating Buddy Hanes since the beginning of the year, but sometimes I felt as if we'd known each other forever. Buddy is a real dynamo—on the swim team, captain of varsity track. Everything comes easily to him, so he just naturally takes a lot for granted—including me.

Leona gave me one of those funny looks that told me she was on the verge of asking me something I might not like. I was right.

"Are you really in love with Buddy?" she asked.

"Kick me in the shins for saying so, but it just seems like you two are just, I don't know—too perfect, somehow. Like you never fight. And you always know where he's taking you on Saturday night. It's like pancakes and maple syrup."

"What?"

I shouldn't have been surprised, really. Leona was always coming up with these strange ideas. Like the time she dared me at one of our slumber parties to go down to the corner grocery in my pajamas for Oreos and milk. I did it, but Leona said it was cheating because I wore my coat.

"OK," she said. "What do you think of when someone says pancakes? Maple syrup, right? It's like you always know when you eat pancakes, you're going to put maple syrup on top."

"Leona, what are you talking about?"

"Pancakes with peanut butter and whipped cream!" she cried, flinging her arms out. "Pancakes and rocky road ice cream! I don't know—anything—something different. Something exciting and unpredictable. Isn't that what being in love is supposed to be all about?"

"I never heard being in love compared to pancakes and peanut butter."

"Well, do you know what I mean or don't you?"

I sighed. "Yeah, well, I guess in the fireworks

department, Buddy and I aren't exactly up there with you and Sid."

Leona and her boyfriend, Sid, were always either in the middle of a fight or making up—usually right in the middle of a corridor during the lunch-hour rush. I'd never known one of their break-ups to last more than a couple of hours.

Leona grinned sheepishly. "Well, at least no one could ever accuse us of being boring."

"That's for sure!"

"Look, Joy," Leona said as she looped an affectionate arm around my shoulders, "I'm sorry if it seems like I'm getting on your case. I guess it really is none of my business. I just want to be sure you're really happy, that's all."

I thought about it for a minute, then said, "Well, at least I don't think I'm *un*happy."

"Do Buddy's kisses set you on fire?"

"Leona!"

"Well, do they?"

"Leona, stop it!"

We were both laughing so hard we could hardly walk straight. Mrs. Ryan passed by us and gave us one of those I-don't-know-what-you're-up-to-but-I-don't-like-it looks. Then she glanced at her wristwatch with a little flip of her wrist.

"You'd better hurry, girls," she said. "Class will be starting any second."

"Do you think Mr. Ryan's kisses ever set Mrs. Ryan on fire?" I whispered to Leona when she was gone.

"Sure they do," Leona said, trying to keep a straight face. But her lips were twitching like crazy, and tears of wild laughter were forming in the corners of her eyes. "Just like the burning of Atlanta in *Gone With The Wind*."

"Leona, you're hopeless," I said, laughing. "Positively hopeless!"

Our laughter died down slowly, and as we walked along to class, I thought about what Leona had said about Buddy and me. She was right, I realized, though I hated to admit it—my relationship with Buddy *was* a little on the boring side. We didn't really excite each other all that much, for one thing, in spite of the fact that we hardly ever argued. And, also, his kisses didn't exactly compare with the burning of Atlanta. A good marshmallow-toasting fire, maybe. But I liked it that way—or so I was told myself. Our relationship was safe, no surprises.

Surprises make me nervous.

Chapter Four

"Surprise!" my mother had cried the day she came home from work and announced that we were moving to Piper's Point.

We were living with Grandpa in Seattle then, in a big, old, off-white frame house on Chestnut Street. Everything was exactly the way I wanted it to be. My best friend, Caroline, lived two houses down the street, and from our block we could walk to school or to the Walgreen's on Saturday to try on makeup and squirt our wrists with perfume. Kevin had a tree fort that Grandpa built in the backyard. Even Buster, our old mutt, had his place: a torn couch cushion wedged in behind the water heater out on the sunporch.

Mom was balancing a pizza box on one hand.

31

She never brought home take-out food unless there was reason for a celebration.

"I got a job!" she said. "I mean, a better job!" Her cheeks were all pink, and with her hair pulled back in a ponytail, she looked about sixteen. She put the pizza box down and slung one arm around Kevin and one around me. "Look, guys, it means we'll have to move out of Seattle, but it's a hundred dollars more a week. A hundred dollars! Maybe we can even afford to buy a new car now. Or at least get the station wagon fixed so it doesn't keep breaking down."

"What about Grandpa?" I asked suspiciously. "Is he coming with us?"

"Yeah," Kevin chimed. "And Buster, too?"

As if he knew we were talking about him, Buster trotted over and gave the pizza a tentative sniff. He usually loves pizza, but that time he turned away with a mournful look.

"Buster can come," Mom said, casting a quick glance at Grandpa. "Of course, Buster can come." But she didn't say anything about Grandpa. I knew then that they had already talked about it and that it had already been pretty much decided.

In the end the hardest part of moving was leaving Grandpa. It was even harder than saying goodbye to Caroline, who cried buckets of tears and gave me a desk set with a poodle penholder so I could write to her every other day. Grandpa didn't say much at all, except that he thought it was a good thing. Besides the money, I think he figured it was time for Mom to start living her own life.

Three years before, when my dad had died, Mom wouldn't even leave the house to go to a movie. Grandpa was always pushing her, telling her, "Go, go. Go bowling, anything, just get out of my sight!" He sounded like he was being mean, but it was only because he loved her. So I knew why he thought it was a good thing that she was finally moving out on her own. Even though good things sometimes hurt—a lot.

"Get out of here," Grandpa said when it was time to go. He gave me a playful little shove as I carried the last of the boxes out to the car. "You think I'm going to miss you, don't you? Well, let me tell you, I can't wait for the bunch of you to clear out so I can finally have some peace and quiet around here."

His eyes were wet, and there was a funny wobble in his voice. I hugged him hard so that he wouldn't see that I was trying not to cry, too.

"I'll phone all the time. And we'll visit sometimes," I said.

"Better make the calls collect. Don't want you using up all that new-car money on phone calls."

"Grandpa," I asked, "are you really glad we're leaving?" Of course I already knew the answer, but I wanted to hear it anyway.

"What do you think, Mutt?" He was always calling Kevin and me Mutt and Jeff after some comic strip characters that used to be popular a long time ago.

I looked up at him. There were flakes of pipe tobacco clinging to his collar. He looked older than he ever had before. His eyes were so faded you could hardly tell they were blue.

"I think," I said slowly, "that you'll miss me as much as I'm going to miss you."

"Ha!" he grunted. But it was a nice grunt.

He hugged me back, so hard I could feel my bones crack.

Then I was squashed into the backseat of the station wagon between two overflowing cartons, with Buster's tail whacking me between the shoulder blades. I waved goodbye until Grandpa dissolved into a distant, watery speck.

That was just the first of all the changes that were to come.

I got home at about 4:30, after spending some time at Leona's listening to her new Police album. As I walked in the door, I could hear someone banging away in the kitchen, so I knew Paul was home. Paul is a carpenter, and when he's not at work building people's houses, he fixes things around our house. Right then he was in the process of remodeling the kitchen—a sort of wedding present to Mom.

In order to get to the refrigerator, I had to step around lots of tools. An electrical cord snaked its way out from the table. My sneakers left waffled prints in the sawdust that covered the floor like fine snow.

Paul grinned when he saw me. "Hey, kid, how's it going?"

I don't really mind it when he calls me kid because I know he doesn't mean anything by it. He even calls Mom kid sometimes, which is really funny. It's just his way.

"It's going," I answered. My standard response.

Faced with a choice between an apple, a slice of ham, and some leftover macaroni and cheese, I took the apple.

"Glad to hear it," Paul said. "Well"—he tapped the new cabinet he'd just finished installing over the sink—"what do you think so far?"

"She'll love it."

I bit into the apple. Then I examined the bit-out part. Once when I was about six I bit into an apple, and when I looked down, one of my front teeth was stuck in it. So now it's a habit. I always look after the first bite.

"Yeah, well, you know it's yours, too." Paul was scratching his beard as he looked at me, his blue eyes serious. "What do you say I start on your room next? You could use some extra closet space."

I shrugged. "OK by me."

I suppose I should've acted more excited, but it was hard getting used to this business of Paul building himself right into our lives, cupboard by cupboard, closet by closet. I wondered if things were about to get awkward.

I was rescued at that moment by Kev, who came bursting in through the back door as if he'd been shot out of a cannon. Kevin was ten—the age, Mom says, when a person has more energy than he knows what to do with.

"Hi, Paul! Hey, what are you doing? Looks

36

great! Can I help? Would you show me how to do that stuff?"

Talk poured out of Kevin in a nonstop stream. Sometimes he reminds me of one of those wind-up dolls, except that he never winds down completely.

Paul rumpled Kevin's hair, which is a pure carrot red. He's got freckles, too.

"Sure, pal. Grab that sack of nails over there. I could use an extra pair of hands right now."

Kev's face lit up as if he'd just been knighted or something. He really worshipped Paul. My brother couldn't wait until Mom and Paul got married so Paul could officially be his stepdad. They had a nice, easy relationship—no hassles, no hitches. Sometimes I envied them—I wished I could let go and allow things to just be. Then there were other times when the two of them really bugged me—especially Kevin, for being so easily won over.

"I've got to make a phone call," I muttered before ducking out of the kitchen.

I could have saved my breath. Kev and Paul were so busy talking they didn't even notice my leaving.

I dialed Grandpa's number on the hall extension.

"Hi, Grandpa?"

"Mutt! What're you doing calling me this time of day? You should've waited until tonight when the rates are cheaper. Does your mother know you're calling?" His voice seemed to be coming through layers of crackling tissue paper.

"Don't worry, Grandpa, I'm paying for it myself. I have some baby-sitting money saved up."

"Well, now, it's sure nice to know you're so well off. Maybe you should've just hopped in your Rolls-Royce and driven on down to see me instead of calling."

"Sorry, Grandpa, but I gave my chauffeur the day off. We'll see you soon, though."

He laughed. "So how're you doing otherwise?"

"OK."

"Just OK? Remember, your mom didn't name you Joy for nothing. You have a fight with that boyfriend of yours? Is that what this is all about?"

"No! Buddy and I are fine. I just felt like saying hi, that's all."

"Funny time of the day to be calling for that."

I giggled. "Would you like it better if I told you the whole family had come down with the bubonic plague?"

38

"Now that'd be something worth calling about."

We talked for another five minutes or so, just joking back and forth. It was always good to hear his voice even though we weren't really saying anything important. I still missed seeing Grandpa every day—even after all this time. I was glad he'd be coming up for the wedding.

As far as I was concerned, it was the only good thing about the wedding that I could think of.

Chapter Five

"There's going to be a body in that closet, I just know it," I hissed, covering my face with my hands.

We were watching a double feature at the Skyview Drive-In—*Friday the 13th, II* and *Motel Mania.* Buddy's idea, not mine. I hate gory movies.

Buddy nudged me with his elbow. "You're missing the best part."

Beth leaned over the front seat, whispering in my ear, "Just keep telling yourself it's not real blood. That's what I do. They use catsup, I think."

"No, they don't, ding-dong," said her boyfriend, Peter. "If they used catsup, they'd have to deep fry the bodies first."

Beth socked his arm. "How can anyone be so gross?"

Beth and Peter have been going together since the beginning of time, I think. Even so, they acted more like brother and sister than steadies. Still, they were more fun to double-date with than Leona and Sid, who usually spent the whole time either fighting or making up.

Buddy tightened his arm around my shoulders. "Don't worry," he murmured. "If a psycho like that ever came after you, I'd protect you."

"Thanks," I said, "I'd do the same for you."

He gave me a funny look. Obviously he couldn't imagine me giving some guy a karate chop in the windpipe.

Peter was hamming it up royally in the backseat, making weird noises and scrunching up his face in his best imitation of a maniac on the loose. Beth was giggling and punching his arm playfully, telling him to knock it off.

"Shhh," hissed Buddy. *Motel Mania* was coming on. "This is a good one. It's about this real creepy motel where they drug the guests and then plant them in rows with just their heads sticking up. Like cabbages."

I moaned. "Sounds charming. Come on,

Buddy, can't we go? I've seen enough blood for one night."

Beth was on my side. "There's a new group playing down at Corky's. I hear they're pretty good."

Corky's is a pizza-burger place where most of the kids from school hang out. Their food isn't all that fantastic, but they have live music every Wednesday and Saturday night.

"Yeah," Peter said in his Igor voice. "I have a sudden craving for french-fried fingers."

That did it. Even Buddy couldn't watch the movie with a straight face after that. So we ended up going to Corky's after all. Unfortunately we weren't the only ones who decided to go there that night. The place was wall-to-wall people. We looked for seats, but all the booths were filled.

A curly, dark head bobbed up from one of the booths. Someone was waving an arm and yelling at us.

Buddy grinned and waved back. "Hey, Richie!"

Beth and I looked at each other. I groaned. "Oh, no."

The trouble with being Buddy's girlfriend was that he and Richie were friends—not best friends or anything, but they hung out together.

Wherever I turned, it seemed, Richie was popping up. I avoided him whenever I could, but that time there was no getting around it. Buddy had me by the wrist and was dragging me over to where Richie was sitting.

"I see you brought your groupies along, big shot," Richie said teasingly, his eyes twinkling at Beth and me as we squeezed in after Buddy. Peter sat down next to Richie.

It was just the kind of macho remark you'd expect from a guy like Richie. In a loud voice I said to Beth, "Don't mind him. Normally he wears a straitjacket; so if he seems a little strange, you'll have to forgive him."

Richie raised his root beer mug to me. "Touché, J.W."

Before I could say anything, the waitress came over. After we had ordered a pizza and drinks, I glared at Richie. "Will you stop calling me J.W.?"

"What's wrong with it? It suits you. Short but sweet."

Just for the record, I'm five-four, which isn't really all that short, but I could see how I must've looked from Richie's six-foot vantage point. I could feel myself turning red.

Buddy wore a mystified expression. "I don't

get it. Why are you two always at each other's throats?"

Buddy is the kind of person who thinks that the people he likes should automatically like each other, too. How Buddy and Richie ended up being friends, I'll never know.

Physically, they're opposites, too. Richie is tall, dark, and on the lean side. Buddy is the muscle-bound type, with a thick shock of blond hair curving down over one eye.

Peter was back to hamming it up, this time as Dracula. "So you vant to know vy they're always at each other's throats, huh?"

"Ask *him*," I said, jabbing a finger at Richie. "He's the one who's always starting it."

"Who, me?" Richie asked with mock incredulity. His face smoothed into an innocent mask. "All I have to do is say hello, and she jumps all over me."

"Ha!" I exclaimed, using one of Grandpa's favorite expressions.

"See what I mean? I can't do anything right as far as she's concerned." Richie put on a stricken look while he pressed his hand to his chest. "Doomed to a Joy-less existence!"

This latest witticism of his was greeted by a round of snickers, while I sat there fuming.

44

"Uh-oh," said Peter, glancing over at me. "Looks like you hit the bull's-eye that time, Rich."

By then, everybody at our table was cracking up, including Buddy. Not wanting to be accused of having a subzero sense of humor, I forced a smile.

"Macho-man strikes again," I said to Beth, loud enough for everyone to hear.

"Hey, I heard that," Richie said. "Watch who you call a chauvinist, will you?"

"I'll bet he doesn't even know the meaning of the word," said Beth, happily getting into the battle.

"What can you expect from someone who was swinging from branch to branch until yesterday?" I replied sweetly.

Richie frowned, and I knew I'd hit my mark. "Hey, no fair. The trouble with some of you girls is that you think just because a guy opens a door for you he's out to get you."

I giggled. "What about when he slams it in your face?"

Richie shook his head. "I pity the poor guy who gets stuck with you, J.W. He won't know whether he's coming or going."

At that point Buddy slung an arm about my

shoulders. "I'll take the consequences," he said, planting a kiss on the end of my nose.

I could feel Richie's eyes boring into me again. The way he was staring, I felt like an amoeba under a microscope. Suddenly I couldn't sit still a moment longer. I squirmed my way out of the booth.

"Come on, Buddy, let's dance," I said.

He shook his head. Our pizza had just arrived, steaming and fragrant from the oven. "Naw, let's eat first. I'm hungry." He lifted a dripping wedge to his mouth.

Richie motioned for Peter to move so that he could get out of the booth. "Never fear, once again Sir Richard rides to the rescue. I'll dance with you, J.W.—just to show you I'm not a total clod."

Before I could protest, he'd grabbed me by the elbow and was steering me toward the dance floor. At the last minute, I snatched my arm away.

"I don't feel like dancing anymore," I told him.

"Try it. You never know, you might like it."

"That's what my mother used to tell me about creamed spinach."

"Mine, too. But, listen, they were right. It grows on you—it really does."

"I still hate it."

"Well, don't worry," he said, clamping an arm around my waist and propelling me onto the dance floor. "I promise I don't taste anything like creamed spinach."

It was like the time he kissed me. I couldn't believe it was happening—that I was actually dancing with Richie Brennan. Actually, to tell the truth, he wasn't a bad dancer. His movements blended with the music, light and easy. Some guys get you into a wrestler's clinch; other guys are so afraid to get near you, they hold you like you'd melt if they breathed too hard on you. I also hate the ones who steer you around like they're driving a car at seventy miles an hour.

Richie wasn't John Travolta, but like I said, he was pretty good. He held me at just the right distance, and his hands, even though warm, didn't sweat through my blouse. I felt myself growing warm, too.

I guess that's what bothered me the most—the fact that my body didn't seem to hate Richie as much as my mind did.

When the song ended, I pulled away from him as if I'd just been sprung loose from a bear trap.

"Thanks," I muttered.

"Don't mention it, J.W."

Giving me a grin he spun off into the crowd, and I saw him sit down with a group of kids at another table. I went back and ate three slices of mushroom-and-pepper pizza that I didn't really want and ended up feeling sick to my stomach. It wasn't turning out to be one of the best nights of my life. I couldn't stop thinking about Richie and the strange way I had felt about him while we were dancing.

All in all, I think I would have been better off sticking it out through *Motel Mania*.

Chapter Six

The results of the senior poll appeared in Friday's edition of *The Cabrillo Call*. This issue was the only one of the year that all the students read, and since there were never enough papers printed, people had to fight one another to get a look at the poll results. I was outside heading back to school after a free period when Torey and Leona came flying down the ramp toward me. Leona was waving *The Call* over her head like a banner.

"Joy! You're in it, you're in it!" Torey was yelling at the top of her lungs. She pushed the paper right in front of my face.

At first I didn't see my name. I noticed that Torey had been named Prettiest, just as we thought she would. Leona had lost out on Funniest to Alma Lewis. That one I found pretty hard to believe. Alma is the kind of person who goes around telling elephant jokes, and for her yearbook picture last year she stuck her tongue out at the last second, just as the photographer was snapping the shot. Personally, I think the school should have created a new category so Alma could have been selected Weirdest.

I noticed that Buddy had been chosen Most Athletic, along with Lisa Horsnyder, who could run the fifty-yard dash faster than anyone in school. And Malcolm had gotten Most Likely to Succeed. No surprise there.

Then I saw it.

Best Companion on a Desert Island—Joy Wilder and . . . *Richie Brennan.*

I stared at the print in disbelief. Was this some kind of horrible joke? Normally I would have been thrilled to get what was considered the top prize in the poll, but sharing it with Richie was not my idea of terrific. It meant we would have to pose for pictures together for one thing. I hoped they wouldn't make us do something gross like hold hands. Last year, for the same category, Kenny Lassiter and Brenda Soloman posed kissing, but I figured that had more to do with the fact that they were going together than anything else.

50

"Is it too late to back out?" I wondered aloud.

Torey and Leona exchanged glances.

"Look, Joy," Leona said, "I know how you feel about sharing it with Richie, but that's dumb. It's not as though they're saying you have to really be stuck on a desert island with him or anything."

Torey sighed. "*I* wouldn't mind being stuck on an island with Richie."

"Good," I said. "You can have him then!"

Leona giggled. "It *would* be romantic. Just like Brooke Shields and Chris Atkins in *The Blue Lagoon*."

"More like Robinson Crusoe and the cannibals," I said.

"Come on," said Leona. "You're blowing this whole thing out of proportion, aren't you?"

"What thing?"

"This whole thing between Richie and you. Why not just ignore him if you don't like him?"

"That's like me telling you to ignore Godzilla while he's stomping on your house."

"Come on, you're exaggerating!" Torey laughed.

She squinted at a group of boys who were passing by. Torey is terribly nearsighted, but she won't wear glasses unless she's in class and has to read what's on the blackboard. I'm glad

I'm not as pretty as Torey. I'd feel like I could never really relax and be comfortable. Not that Torey is really all that uptight, but, for instance, the time all four of us went shopping at a classy mall, Torey wore high heels and wouldn't change into the pair of sneakers she'd bought even though she had blisters and could hardly walk. She was afraid people would stare at her if she was wearing Adidas with her good dress. I would've worn the Adidas and not have cared if I'd looked like a clown.

One of the boys had separated himself from the group and was walking toward us. He had a camera slung around his neck. Our resident photographer, Sandy Cortland.

Torey, Leona, and I took one look at each other and headed as quickly as we could in the opposite direction. Sandy was always snapping candid shots of us, some of which had turned up in previous yearbooks. There was one of Torey eating a sandwich with a big hunk of bologna hanging out of her mouth. When she first saw it, she asked very calmly if we thought murdering Sandy would be considered justifiable homicide in a court of law. Sandy also took a shot of me cheerleading in the rain at a football game. In that picture my hair was plastered to my head in funny little ringlets and my cheeks were streaked with mascara. Beth and Leona were huddled behind me, looking just as miserable. So you can see why we weren't glad to run into Sandy.

"Hey, guys, wait up!" Sandy called as he dashed after us, his camera banging against his chest. He never gives up. "No pictures, I promise!"

I slowed and looked over at Leona. "Should we trust him?"

"Do you have a mirror?" Leona asked. "Before I answer that, I want to check to make sure I don't have anything stuck between my teeth."

"Do I look all right?" Torey asked, patting her hair.

By that time Sandy had caught up with us.

He pointed at his camera. "Don't worry, it's not loaded," he said, as if it were a pistol he was talking about. "You can relax."

"Make one false move and you're a dead man," Leona growled in her best imitation of a gun-slinger.

"Is this the face of a liar?" he asked, giving us his most beguiling look.

"Yes!" we chorused.

Sandy doesn't look like a troublemaker, but

we all knew better. You would think he would've built up more muscles from lugging around all those cameras, but he's as skinny as a toothpick. The thickest part of him is his hair, which is brown and bushy and sticks out all over his head.

"OK," said Torey, giving him a threatening look. "But if you try anything, we'll never speak to you again."

Not much of a threat, in my opinion. Sandy grinned, and I knew what he was probably thinking: one picture is worth a thousand words.

"Hey," he said, "don't be so suspicious. I just wanted to congratulate you on the senior poll."

"You, too, Joy," he said. "That's what I wanted to talk to you about. I have this fantastic idea for the yearbook layout. I already talked it over with Richie, and he thinks it's great, too."

Instantly I was on my guard. "What is it?"

"The island thing is perfect, don't you think? I mean, look at all the islands we've got around here. So, I thought, wouldn't it be great if I could get some shots of you two on a *real* island—"

"Huh-uh, no way. Not me." I started backing up. If my friends hadn't stopped me, I would've backed right into a tree.

"Why not?" Sandy wanted to know. "It's a great idea! Just give me one good reason why you're against it."

"I'll give you one. Richie Brennan."

"Oh, that." Sandy shook his head. "Yeah, Richie told me you'd probably say that."

"He did?" I could feel heat climbing into my cheeks. "What else did he say?"

Now it was Sandy's turn to back up. "Uh, well, nothing much, really. He just said you probably weren't the type who would want to spend a day roughing it outdoors on some crummy island, anyway."

"He told you that?" My voice was at least three octaves higher than normal. "He told you I was too much of a sissy to rough it?"

"He didn't exactly put it that way—"

"Well, you can just tell him right back that I can out-rough him any day!"

"How about proving it instead?" he suggested. "Tomorrow. The harbor at eleven. My uncle has a boat he's letting me use."

Before I knew what I was doing, I found myself agreeing. Sandy doesn't look it, but like I said, he's dangerous.

"Don't worry, Joy," Torey said, patting my shoulder sympathetically. "I'm sure it won't be so bad. It's only for an afternoon. What can happen in an afternoon?"

A lot, I thought. When it came to Richie Brennan, anything was possible.

Chapter Seven

Paul was fixing breakfast when I got up Saturday morning.

"Want some pancakes?" he asked.

I shook my head. "No thanks."

I could see he had gone to a lot of trouble, and I felt a twinge of guilt. He had a dish towel tucked in the waist of his pants, but the front of his shirt was covered with flour.

"I'm going boating today," I explained. "I'm afraid I might get seasick if I eat too much. I'll just have some toast."

Kevin was busy stuffing his face with pancakes at the table. "Look at me, I'm the pancake shark."

It was a game we used to play a lot when we were younger. Whenever something disappeared from the refrigerator, one of us would say, "The cake shark must have eaten it," or maybe it was the fried-chicken shark or the ice-cream shark. Personally I thought Kevin was getting a little old for that game.

"You shouldn't take such big bites," I told him as I sat down to eat my toast. "It's gross for other people to have to watch."

"Then don't watch," he said, stuffing an entire pancake into his mouth.

"Yuck!" I turned sideways in my chair.

Something cold and wet touched my hand. It was Buster's nose. I fed him half my toast, which was burned anyway.

"Are you on a diet?" Kevin asked. He was staring straight at my stomach.

I balled up my napkin and tossed it at him. "Shut up, you little creep!"

"Joy!"

My mother stood in the doorway. She was wearing a pretty yellow robe, one I hadn't seen before. She had a whole collection of new robes now. In the old days, before Paul moved in, she always wore the same one, an old chenille robe with most of the fuzz worn off. She didn't always fix her hair before she came to breakfast, either. Now it fell in shiny, butter-colored waves around her shoulders. Even with no makeup on, she looked pretty.

She came over and sat down next to me. "OK, kiddo, I don't mind a bad mood now and then. We all have them, heaven knows, but you've been biting our heads off since yesterday. Want to tell me what's wrong?"

At that moment I wanted nothing more than to lay my head against her shoulder, the way I used to when I was a lot younger. I could tell her anything then. But not anymore. It would've seemed too babyish, especially in front of Paul and Kevin. Besides, nothing had been the same since Paul. A few months before I'd put my head against my mother's shoulder, just for a second, and I had smelled Paul's after-shave.

"Nothing's wrong," I lied.

She smiled. Her eyes are really beautiful when she smiles—they get all shiny and kind of crinkle up at the corners. They're grayish-green, like mine, only hers are less gray and more green, the color of freshly watered leaves.

She knew I was lying, and somehow that made me feel even worse.

"OK," she said and sighed, "have it your way. I guess you'll tell me when you're ready."

"She's on a diet," Kevin said with his mouth full. "That's why she's so uptight."

"I am not!" I protested.

"Enough, you two," Mom said, pressing her hands against her temples. "Can't you at least wait until I've had my coffee?"

"Coming right up, ma'am." Paul set a steaming mug in front of her.

"Thanks, sweetheart." She gazed up at him. Their eyes locked, and suddenly it was as if Kevin and I had disappeared into thin air.

I always get this funny feeling in the pit of my stomach when they look at each other that way. Part of it, I know, is jealousy because I hate being excluded from what is obviously a major part of Mom's life. But also it's the way I like to imagine someone will look at *me* someday.

You see, I'm actually very romantic under the surface. I went to see *An Officer And A Gentleman* three times, and I cried each time at the end when Richard Gere picks up Debra Winger and carries her out of the factory. I can't really picture some guy carrying me like that, but it's a nice thought, anyway. If for some reason Buddy had to carry me, he'd probably sling me over his shoulder like a sack of flour. If Richie . . .

I stopped myself. Why was I thinking about

him? It was bad enough that I was being practically forced into spending the whole day with him. How had I gotten myself into this mess?

Paul and Mom had unglued their eyes from each other. Now Paul was looking over at me.

"We've been talking about having the ceremony in the chapel garden instead of indoors," he said. "What do you think, Joy?"

"What if it rains?" I asked. The weather in Piper's Point, especially in the spring, can be pretty unpredictable.

Besides, I sort of resented him asking my opinion about something he and my mom had probably already made up their minds about anyway. I knew he was only asking me so I would feel included in their plans.

"I'll carry an umbrella instead of a bouquet," Mom said, laughing.

"I'll build a bower," Paul said. "We can stand under that."

Obviously he didn't care if the rest of us got soaked.

"Hey, neat, can I help build it?" Kevin piped up.

"Sure thing, pal." Paul reached over and rumpled his hair.

"What about Grandpa?" I asked. "Shouldn't

we ask him what he thinks about the ceremony being outside?"

"Well, I don't know," Mom said, staring out of the window as she fidgeted with her coffee spoon. "It was just a thought, anyway."

I couldn't think of anything to say, so I quickly fed the rest of my toast to Buster, then excused myself from the table. Before I left the room, I turned and looked at my family. Kevin was on his third stack of pancakes. Pretty soon he would be up to the record Paul had set. Mom was flipping through an L.L. Bean catalog—she and Paul were going camping up in Canada for their honeymoon—while Paul poured the last of the batter onto the griddle in one long, sizzling stream.

All at once I couldn't wait to escape. Even the thought of spending the afternoon with Richie didn't seem so terrible anymore.

Sandy was waiting at the dock when I arrived. There were two cameras slung around his neck instead of his usual one. It was a hot day, so he was wearing shorts. I couldn't help noticing how white his legs were, almost as white as the Styrofoam cooler he was sitting on.

"Richie's going to be a little late," Sandy announced. "He had to take his sister to her flute lesson."

"Oh." Somehow, I'd never thought of Richie as having a life outside of school, complete with a home and family obligations.

After a few minutes, Richie came swinging down the splintery old dock with a duffel bag slung over one suntanned shoulder. He was wearing jogging shorts, and his legs were brown and muscular. He waved when he spotted us.

"Hi," I said, not wanting to start out on the wrong foot.

Speaking of which, he was staring down at my feet. "You should've worn sneakers," Richie said. "Some of those islands are pretty rocky. Those sandals won't be much good for climbing."

"I'm not worried," I said, resentment already simmering inside me.

He shrugged. "It's not my problem. I was just trying to be helpful."

"It must be nice being the world's biggest expert on everything," I commented.

Richie laughed. "You always manage to get in the last word, don't you?"

I suppose I should have felt flattered that

Richie considered me capable of getting the better of him, but instead I felt vaguely let down. I avoided his eyes, which looked bluer than ever contrasted against the tan he'd acquired the past few sunny days.

"Well, shall we hit the water, folks?" Sandy took a deep breath before hefting the cooler under one arm.

We followed him down a short flight of swaying steps to where his uncle's motorboat was tied up. It wasn't one of those big fancy boats shaped like a bullet, with speed to match. This one was barely large enough for the three of us and Sandy's equipment. The paint was peeling off the sides, and it smelled like cod liver oil inside. Sandy had trouble getting the motor started, but finally it sputtered to life, and we were off.

The water was calm, and it sparkled like ice. People think the ocean this far north is always really cold, but in the strait it sometimes gets up to seventy-five degrees in the summer—as warm as in Hawaii. It has something to do with a current that flows up from Japan—I think.

Richie stood at the front of the boat, with his hand shading his eyes against the sun, looking like some kind of Viking warrior. The wind ruffled his hair into little peaks. I wondered what he was thinking.

We circled around a few islands before we found one that looked right for picture taking. There was a high bluff we could stand on while Sandy snapped shots from the boat with his telephoto lens. There was also what was left of a dock—a couple of pilings we could tie up to. Someone must have lived there at one time; up ahead, through the trees, I could see a broken-down old ruin of a cabin.

"Let's eat before we start," Richie suggested. "I'm starved."

We spread a couple of beach towels over the rocks and polished off the food Sandy had brought in the cooler—some chicken salad sandwiches, oatmeal cookies, and a thermos of iced tea. Afterward Sandy took two or three shots of seagulls in order to use up what was left of the film in his camera. Then he started fumbling around in his case for an extra roll.

"I know I brought it," he mumbled, getting more frantic and red as the minutes passed. "It has to be in here somewhere." At that point, though, it seemed pretty obvious that it wasn't in there anywhere.

I couldn't believe what was happening. I had

come all the way out there for nothing. We searched in the boat and on the rocks to make sure the film hadn't fallen out somehow, but we all knew that was pretty unlikely.

"Look, guys," Sandy finally said, "I could go back and get some film. It wouldn't take me more than an hour. You could even catch some rays while I'm gone."

I was on the verge of calling the whole thing off right then and there when I remembered that Paul and my mother were planning to go shopping for new wallpaper that afternoon, and I would probably be roped into going with them if I got home too early.

"You look like you could use a little sun," Richie said, his glance taking in my legs below the line of my navy shorts. They weren't as white as Sandy's, but they were a close second.

"I didn't bring any suntan lotion," I snapped.

"No problem," Richie said, reaching into his duffel bag. "You can borrow mine."

I couldn't think of a comeback to that, so I kept my mouth shut. Sandy had taken off his shoes and was slogging his way back out to the boat.

"See you in a couple of weeks!" he called back

to us, adding with a grin, "Just kidding! I'll be back before you know I'm gone!"

You'd better be, I thought, glancing over at Richie. I didn't know how long we could be alone together without killing each other.

Chapter Eight

"You should've brought a sweater or something," Richie said. We'd been waiting over an hour, and it was starting to get windy.

"I didn't think of it. Anyway, I'm not all that cold," I retorted. An obvious lie, since there was no way to disguise the goosebumps that covered my arms and legs.

Richie untied the arms of his nylon jacket, which was knotted around his waist. He handed it to me. "Here," he said, "put this on." It was more of an order than an offer.

"No, thanks. I don't need it." At that moment I would have frozen to death before I put on his crummy jacket.

"Well, if being stubborn is more important to you than getting warm, be my guest," he said. "Personally, I think you're being ridiculous."

I glared at him. "Who asked you for your opinion? Why don't you just leave me alone?"

"That might be pretty hard to do since there's no way for me to leave."

"Well, Sandy should be back any minute," I said, "and then we can both leave."

"Don't count on it." Richie squinted out at the ocean. "Look how choppy it's gotten. There must be a storm brewing. See those clouds over there on the horizon? Thunderclouds."

"I know what thunderclouds look like," I snapped. Then, a minute later, I asked in a much more subdued voice, "Are you sure?"

I didn't particularly like the looks of things, either. As I said, spring weather in Washington can change suddenly. One minute the sun is shining and there's not a cloud in the sky, then the next minute rain is pelting down.

"I'm not the weatherman," Richie said, "but I'll bet anything we're in for it."

I groaned. "I don't believe it. I don't believe this is happening."

It was like one of those ancient curses: every time I got within ten feet of Richie, disaster was sure to strike.

"Look, it's not the end of the world," he pointed out with infuriating cheerfulness. "We

69

can stick it out until it blows over. The worst thing that can happen is we'll get a little wet." He grinned at me. "Come on, where's your pioneer spirit? You're not afraid of a little rain, are you, J.W.?"

I ignored that one. I was too miserable to rise to the bait. A storm meant that Sandy wouldn't be returning until . . . who knew how long it might take? What if Sandy had been ship-wrecked? No one would ever find us. We'd be stuck there for the next fifty years. A hundred years from now they would find our bones bleaching on those very rocks. . . .

I was really getting myself worked up imagining the worst, when I was jolted back to reality by something splashing over my legs.

"Run for it!" Richie cried as he dashed toward the trees.

I was having a hard time keeping up with him because my sandals kept slipping on the rocks. I wished I'd worn my sneakers. Knowing Richie had been right about that got me even more furious at him.

We made it to the cabin just in time. A minute later, the whole sky seemed to cave in. Of course, the cabin wasn't much protection with half the roof missing, but it was better than nothing.

"The trick is not to think about it," Richie said. He crouched down next to where I sat shivering on a pile of old newspapers, my knees pulled in against my chest.

"About what?"

"The rain. Whenever I'm in a bad situation, I think about someplace I'd rather be."

"That's easy. I can think of a million other places I'd rather be right now."

A slow smile spread across his face. "How about a pizza parlor? Where the windows are all steamed up and the cheese just slides right off the crust when you pick up your slice."

That kind of talk was making me hungry. It hadn't been all that long since we'd eaten, but just the thought of missing dinner was enough to make my stomach growl.

"I wish we had a fire," I said. "Then we could at least dry out."

"We don't have any matches," he said. "Besides, where would we find dry wood?"

"I didn't say we *could*. I just said I *wished* we could."

"OK, you don't have to yell at me."

"I wasn't yelling!"

"You are now."

"You bet I am! It's because you make me so

mad whenever I'm around you that I can't help yelling!"

"You're mad at the weather, not at me," he pointed out calmly. "Yelling isn't going to stop it from raining."

Suddenly I realized he was right. Well, at least halfway right. I was mad about a lot of things right then besides Richie. Still, knowing he was right only made me more furious at him.

"What do you know?" I shouted. "You think you know so much about me, but you don't know anything!"

"Calm down, J.W. You're getting all worked up about nothing."

"Nothing!" I leaped to my feet, bumping the side of my head against one of the caved-in beams. Tears of pain stung my eyes. "How would you like it if your mother was marrying someone practically young enough to be your brother? How would you like having your whole family turned upside down?"

I raved on for the next five minutes or so. I can't remember half of what I said. I guess I even forgot who I was saying it to. But I do know it felt good to get it out. The funny part was that Richie just sat there, listening intently. He didn't laugh once. He even waited until I had run out of steam before he spoke.

"I think it all depends," he said, looking at me very seriously.

"On what?" I asked, my voice quavering. I rubbed my head where I'd bumped it.

"On whether or not this guy your mom's marrying is nice."

"He's pretty nice, but what's that got to do with it?"

"Well—it's just that I can think of worse things than a nice stepfather who happens to be a little on the young side." He stared at the ground, frowning as he poked at a soggy pile of leaves with a stick. "Like, well—like parents who fight all the time the way mine do."

I realized I was seeing a different side of Richie just then. A not-kidding-around side. It made me so uncomfortable I wanted to run right out of the cabin. It was like finding out the truth about something when you're better off believing the lie.

One thing I've discovered is that most people don't really want to know the truth—including me. Even when we ask for it. It's like when you ask someone whether they think the dress you're wearing makes you look fat or if your new haircut makes your ears stick out—you only want to hear the truth if it's not going to make you feel bad. Or you might have a best friend who says, "You can tell me anything, no matter how terrible," but you know if you told her about all the times you'd thought about kissing her boyfriend she'd probably hate you.

That's sort of how I felt then. For a minute there, I found I wasn't mad at Richie anymore. It was like losing my place in a book and opening it to the wrong page. I didn't know what to say, how to feel. What if his parents were getting a divorce or something? Then I'd have to feel sorry for him. I didn't want to have to feel sorry for Richie. I was too busy feeling sorry for myself.

Richie, I could tell, was embarrassed, too. "Heck, there's lots of worse things," he said, flipping his head back in that cocky old way of his. There was a familiar evil glint in his eye as he added, "Like getting stuck on an island in the middle of nowhere with you."

"You never quit, do you?" I was slowly inching my way back to hating him again.

"Not if I can help it."

"You'd probably make jokes about it if we were starving to death."

"Well, you've got to admit one thing," he said.

"At least we won't die of thirst." He winked. "Or boredom."

"I give up." I sighed. "Richie Brennan, you're impossible. Absolutely impossible!"

Chapter Nine

It was getting dark, and the rain hadn't even begun to let up. If anything, it was worse than ever. Richie unearthed a Hershey bar from his duffel bag. I was hungry, so I didn't argue when he offered me half.

"If I were a magician, I'd snap my fingers and turn this into a big, fat, juicy steak and a baked potato," he said, waving his half in the air before popping it in his mouth.

"Stop it," I said. "You're only making it worse."

"How could it be worse?"

"I don't know, but thinking about all the things you'd rather be doing is just torturing yourself. And me, too."

"I was supposed to go to a party tonight," he said glumly. "I just hope Marcia believes me when I tell her I spent the day marooned on a desert island."

"Marcia Freeman?"

"Yeah."

That surprised me. I never would've picked out Marica Freeman as Richie's type—not in a million years. For one thing, she's very serious. She's on the honor roll and is very big on causes. She's pretty, but wears these big glasses and T-shirts with slogans on them like "No Nukes Is Good Nukes" and "When God Created The World She Did A Pretty Good Job."

"I didn't know you were going out with Marcia," I said.

"I'm not really. We're mostly just friends." He saw that I was smiling and asked, "What's so funny?"

"Nothing." But I was having a hard time keeping a straight face. "It's just that she doesn't really seem like your type, that's all."

"Oh?" He raised an eyebrow. "And just what is my type then—since you're such an expert on the subject?"

I giggled. Maybe it was the lack of food, or maybe I was becoming delirious with panic.

"Oh, I don't know—the type who gets a thrill

out of baking you chocolate-chip cookies—and washing your socks—"

Even in the dark I could see that Richie was turning red. "Hold it. Just hold it right there." He stood up and started pacing around. The rain was pouring in through the holes in the roof, but he didn't seem to notice. He stared at me angrily.

"Number one." He held up his hand, ticking off one finger, and said, "I don't enjoy being stuck here any more than you do. Number two, for someone who hates to be stereotyped, you sure do a lot of it yourself. And number three— you're the stubbornnest, most opinionated—"

I shot up. "I've heard enough of your dumb reasons!" Before I knew what I was doing, I was heading outside.

"Where are you going?" he demanded.

"Anywhere. I don't care. Just as long as I don't have to hang around listening to you."

"You don't have a jacket. You'll get soaked."

"What's it to you?"

"I couldn't care less. I was just pointing it out, that's all."

He tossed me his wadded-up jacket. "Here. Put this on. I don't want anyone accusing me of letting you get pneumonia. Don't worry, you won't die—you're too stubborn to die of anything!" he yelled after me as I stalked out into the pouring rain.

I was so mad, I didn't know where I was going. But I knew I couldn't get too lost on an island that wasn't much bigger than a football field. The trouble was, though, that the island wasn't flat like a football field. It was mostly a jumble of rocks with a few clumps of trees stuck here and there. The rocks were wet, and my feet kept slipping on them. Once I tripped and skinned my knee, but I didn't stop. I just kept climbing. In a funny way the pain felt good. It gave me a good excuse to cry.

I cried all the way to the top of the bluff. I was drenched to the skin, and I didn't know where the rain stopped and my tears began. Finally, I sat down to catch my breath as well as my thoughts, which were all jumbled up.

Mostly what I thought about was Richie. I thought about what he'd said—that I was categorizing him just as much as he had categorized me. I realized then that the reason I'd gotten so mad was because he was right.

Then my thoughts turned to the night we'd

danced: the warm pressure of his hand against my back, the easy way we'd moved together. . . .

I remembered what he'd said about his parents not getting along.

Maybe he wasn't as shallow as I'd always thought he was. Maybe we'd just gotten off on the wrong foot way back in the beginning.

Maybe the reason he made me so mad was because we were more alike than I wanted to admit.

Stubborn, he'd called me. I guess that applied to my feelings about Paul, too. I was too stubborn to stop resenting Paul for the things he couldn't help—like his age, for one thing, loving my mother, for another.

And there I was, too stubborn to admit how cold and miserable and wet I was—too stubborn to go back to the cabin where at least it was semidry.

I got up. Even stubborn people can admit they're wrong once in a while. By that time it was really black, and getting down the bluff was even harder than going up had been. The rocks were slippery with the rain, and I could barely see past the end of my nose.

Then all of a sudden the ground was sliding out from under me, and I was tumbling down over the rocks. Something that felt like cat's claws raked my side. There was a short, sharp burst of pain in my leg. A wave of red washed in front of my eyes. Then everything went dark.

Chapter Ten

The first thing I saw when I came to was the blurred toe of a sneaker. I blinked, trying to bring it into focus, but the next picture I got was of a face very close to mine peering at me with concern.

"Joy, are you—boy, you had me scared half to death!" Richie's voice sounded as if it were coming through layers of cotton.

I tried standing up, but an arrow of pain shot up my leg, forcing me back down again.

"I think I might have broken something," I said weakly.

"Well, if you did, it would darn well serve you right!" His voice was no longer muffled, but it sounded strangely high-pitched, as if he were on the verge of crying.

"Hey, wait a minute, I—"

"Just shut up, and for once do as I say," he ordered. He bent down and scooped me up. "Hold tight. I don't want to drop you. My legs aren't in such great shape at the moment, either."

An image came to my mind just then, and in my semi-delirious state I started to giggle. It was the image of Richard Gere holding Debra Winger in his arms in that last freeze frame of *An Officer And A Gentleman.* I had always thought it would be so romantic, and there I was being carried off by the last boy on earth I would have picked as a candidate for Prince Charming. I must have looked cute, too, all scraped and muddy, my hair hanging in wet clumps.

"If you think it's so funny, you should try it from my end," Richie said. "You're not exactly a featherweight, you know." But the way he said it, I could tell he was relieved I was OK. Well, sort of OK.

"You can put me down," I suggested. "I could try walking."

"Nothing doing," he said, quickly adding, "And in case you're wondering, it's not because I'm trying to prove how macho I am. I just want to get you back in one piece so that I can roast you over the coals for making me go after you in the rain."

"You followed me?"

He cleared his throat. It made a nice rumbly sound with my ears pressed against his chest. "Yeah, well, I did. I just wanted to make sure you'd be OK. It's a good thing I did, too, or you'd be out of luck."

Even with my ankle throbbing like crazy, I felt good curled up against Richie's chest. I listened to his shoes squishing against the wet rocks. My head seemed to be floating far above my body.

"I'm sorry about all this. I'm glad you followed me," I found myself saying.

Richie grunted. "Well, I never thought I'd live to hear you apologize for anything!"

"Even stubborn people have their moments. Ouch!" I yelled as he set me down. In the dark I hadn't noticed that we had reached the cabin.

"Do you really think it's broken?" Richie knelt, cradling my foot in his hands.

"It feels like it's been run over by a steamroller, but maybe it's only a sprain." The flesh around my ankle was beginning to swell. It felt doughy and tender where he touched it.

"It's lucky you weren't hurt worse."

"Oh, I'm pretty tough."

He grinned. "Yeah, I know. So you keep telling me."

"You don't believe me?"

"Listen, if you want to know the truth, I'm not so tough, either. Tough is just one of my many disguises."

"Which one are you wearing now?"

He made an awkward little bow. "Joy Wilder, I'd like to introduce you to the real, the one and only, Richie Brennan."

I giggled. "Nice to meet you. Hey—you didn't call me J.W. that time."

"I thought you didn't like it."

"I don't, but that never stopped you before."

His voice was husky as he leaned toward me. "I guess I figured making you mad was the only way I could get you to pay attention to me."

I felt myself shiver and wondered whether it was from the cold air or his words. "I—I didn't make it very easy for you, I suppose," I admitted. "You were right about one thing. I can be pretty stubborn sometimes."

"I won't argue with that."

"Anyway, I thought you were making fun of me because you didn't like me."

He was silent for a long time. When he finally

spoke, his voice was quiet and thoughtful. "Maybe I liked you too much," he said.

I was shivering pretty hard by then, and when I looked at him, my breath caught with a sobbing little hitch. Suddenly we had our arms around each other, and Richie was kissing me. His lips were warm and gentle. They tasted like rainwater. It was as if something that had been all knotted up inside me was finally coming loose, unraveling in a flood of warmth. I had never felt that way when Buddy kissed me.

When he pulled back, we were both trembling.

"Are you in love with Buddy?" he asked, as if he'd read my thoughts.

"No," I said. I thought about it for another minute, then added, "And I don't think he's really in love with me, either."

"How do you know?"

I smiled. "He never calls me J.W., for one thing."

"OK, J.W., you tell me. Where do we go from here?"

I shook my head. "I can barely believe what's happening right now."

"I know. Me, too." He touched my face. "I was just wondering if—"

"If what?"

"If none of this had happened. If we hadn't gotten stuck on this dumb island—would we ever have found out we liked each other?"

"I guess we'll never know, will we?"

He folded his fingers into a fist and rubbed it gently along my cheek. Then he kissed me again, more passionately than before.

"How do you feel?" he murmured.

"Wonderful."

"I meant your foot."

"Oh, that—it still hurts. When I think about it. I'm pretty sure it's not broken, though."

Unexpectedly he bent over and gave my foot a quick kiss. I must have looked startled because he asked, "Didn't your mother ever do that when you were little? To make it get better faster?"

"Yeah, I guess so. It was so long ago, I can't remember. Besides, you don't remind me of my mother."

"Thank goodness for that." He looked up. "Hey, guess what? It's not raining anymore."

"That's too bad." I snuggled up against him. "Just when I was getting to like it."

Chapter Eleven

"It was just like a fairy tale. Only better— because it really happened." Torey stretched out next to me on the bed, staring dreamily up at the ceiling.

"The part I liked best was when the coast guard came and rescued you. Tell us that part again," urged Beth, sitting cross-legged on the floor.

"It wasn't such a big deal," I said. An obvious lie. I was blushing from head to bandaged foot. "When the coast guardsmen saw I was hurt, they wanted to go back for a stretcher. Richie wouldn't let them. He carried me out to the boat himself."

"Just like in the movies." Torey sighed.

"Yeah, me Tarzan, you Jane," said Leona,

looking up from the copy of *People* magazine she was flipping through.

"Well, it wasn't like that," I said defensively. "In fact, he almost tripped getting into the boat. But by then, somebody else had hold of me under the arms."

I was quiet for a minute, resting my head against the pillows my mother had propped up in a pile behind me. "He—Richie—he's not like I always thought he was. All that macho stuff—it was just an act to cover up the fact that he was nervous around me."

Torey was squinting up at the poster tacked on the wall over my head. "You know, he really *does* look a lot like Rick Springfield."

"How can you see anything without your glasses?" Beth asked, teasingly.

"I just can, that's how. There are some things you don't need glasses to see."

Leona was being practical for a change. "Well, now that he's come out of the closet, so to speak, what are you going to do about it? Are you breaking up with Buddy?"

"Richie and I talked it over," I said. "We decided it was best if we didn't see each other until it was definitely over between Buddy and me."

"When's that going to be?" Beth wanted to know.

"As soon as I tell him," I said. "I just have to find the right moment, that's all. I mean, I know he's not wildly in love with me or anything, but still—it does seem kind of cruel."

"The longer you put it off the harder it's going to be," Leona pointed out. "But I know what you mean. Breaking up is hard, no matter how you feel about the person."

Torey giggled. "You ought to know more than anyone. You and Sid do it at least once a week."

Leona threw one of my stuffed animals at her. "*You* should talk," she teased right back. "If I ever saw you going out with the same boy twice in a row, I'd probably faint!"

Beth was putting on nail polish—a different shade for each fingernail—trying to decide which one she liked best.

"Peter and I will probably still be going together a hundred years from now," she said without looking up. "We'll have to take turns pushing each other around in our wheelchairs."

"Sounds exciting," I said.

"He once told me that if we ever got married, then decided to get a divorce, I'd have to take him as part of the settlement."

We all got a laugh out of that one. It sounded exactly like something Peter would say. But underneath all his kidding around, he loved Beth a lot more than anyone would suspect. No relationship, I have discovered, is as uncomplicated as it seems on the surface.

What kind of relationship would Richie and I have? I wondered. It was still so new and strange that I had a hard time believing the whole episode on the island wasn't just something my delirious brain had cooked up. Had Richie really kissed me? Had I really told him I cared about him? I got embarrassed when I thought about the things I'd said to him. What would happen when we saw each other again? Would we have anything to say to each other?

I was glad I wouldn't have to go to school the next day, which was Monday. My ankle wasn't broken, but I still couldn't walk on it. The swelling had gone down, and in a day or two I'd be able to get around using a cane. Then I would have to face Buddy and tell him the truth. Richie was probably right about us not seeing each other until then, but I couldn't help wishing I could talk to him anyway. Oh, who was I kidding? What I really wanted was to have him put his arms around me and tell me I hadn't imagined the whole thing. I wanted to make sure we would feel the same about each other in broad daylight, now that we were both safe and dry and reasonably sane.

"I think Joy is asleep," I heard Torey say.

I opened my eyes. "No, I'm not. I was just thinking."

She giggled and rolled onto her stomach. "Let me guess. You were contemplating Einstein's theory of relativity, right?"

"Right."

"Did Einstein have blue eyes?" Beth teased.

"What is this, you guys?" I said, bolting upright. "Don't I even get a break for being injured?"

"Seems to me I've heard that somewhere before," Leona said. "Like out of my own mouth. We're just paying you back now for all the times we begged for mercy. Now that you're in love with Richie, you're never going to hear the end of it."

"I never said I was in love with him," I protested.

"Well, what would you call it then?" Leona asked.

I sank back against the pillows and sighed. "I don't know. It's too soon to tell."

"At least you've got to admit you don't hate him anymore."

Yes, I had to admit I was well past that feeling. But it was funny—there had been something nice and predictable about hating Richie. I'd been sure of our relationship. Now I didn't know what would happen between us, and I was a little scared. Maybe that was one of the reasons I wasn't looking forward to breaking up with Buddy. At least with him I'd always known what to expect.

I closed my eyes and without meaning to fell asleep. When I woke up, my friends were gone. A few minutes later Mom came in and sat on my bed. She looked tired, as if the whole island episode had been more of an ordeal for her than for me. Probably it had.

"You look like a different girl from the one I saw yesterday," she said with unmistakable relief in her voice. "Your color is back to normal."

I sneezed. "I wish the rest of me was."

She bent over and kissed me on the forehead. She smelled faintly of sawdust, the smell that had hung over the house ever since Paul had gotten started remodeling. I decided it wasn't such a bad smell.

"You know, you really had us worried," she

said. "When they called and said you'd been hurt, well, I immediately imagined the worst."

At the hospital they'd x-rayed my foot and had given me a thorough examination. Richie'd stayed with me until the very end, even though he must have been horribly uncomfortable in his wet clothes. When it was finally time for me to leave, Mom and Paul dropped him off at his house on our way home.

"Richie's one great kid," Mom was saying, echoing my thoughts. "Paul thinks so, too. The two of them had a long talk out in the hall while you were getting x-rayed."

"They did?" I wondered what they had talked about. Me?

"Paul invited Richie to the wedding, in fact. Is that OK? At the time it seemed natural, but later I got to thinking maybe we should have left it up to you. Do you mind, Joy?"

"I don't care."

But the truth is, I did. I didn't like the idea of Paul arranging my life the way he'd arranged Mom's and Kevin's. What had happened between Richie and me was private and— special. I couldn't bear the thought of anyone else stepping in the way, however good their intentions. Even though I knew I was probably being unfair, I hadn't gotten over my stubbornness about Paul.

At that moment the door to my bedroom flew open. Kevin raced in, threw something down on my bed, then raced out again. I looked down and saw that it was a get-well card. He'd made it himself. On the front he'd drawn a picture of a capsized boat with a boy and a girl floundering nearby, and underneath was a shark eating something that looked like an oversized Frisbee. Inside, he'd written:

TO MY FAVORITE SISTER,
HOPE YOU FEEL BETTER SOON.
FROM THE PIZZA SHARK

"What is this favorite sister business?" I yelled after him even though he probably couldn't hear me. "I'm your only sister!" I was glad he couldn't see that I was grinning.

"Richie called while you were asleep," Mom told me, getting up to straighten the covers. "He just wanted to know how you were doing. Do you want to call him back?"

"Not right now," I said. "Later." My heart was racing, but I tried to act nonchalant.

I really did want to talk to Richie, but like I

said, I was afraid. Would he feel the same about me? What would we say to each other? Had I really fallen in love with him, or was it just a crazy dream?

I closed my eyes, hoping to escape the questions that chased around my head by going back to sleep, but it was no use. Paul's power saw buzzed in some other part of the house like the whine of a persistent mosquito. Besides, I couldn't stop seeing Richie in my mind, his blue eyes alternately tender and mocking. I kept hearing his voice, too. I imagined him saying, *So you think I'm in love with you, huh, J.W.? Well, we'll see about that. . . .*

Chapter Twelve

Breaking up with Buddy turned out to be easier than I thought, even though he seemed genuinely susprised when I reminded him how little we really had in common.

"I always thought we got along pretty well," he said, his expression more confused than hurt.

"We do. I mean, we did. It's not that—it's—oh, Buddy, don't you see? Leona was right."

"What's Leona got to do with it?"

"She said that when a relationship gets too predictable, all the fun goes out of it."

"I always thought we had fun together."

"We did—some of the time. But, well, I guess what I mean to say is that it's not enough if you don't love the person. Do you know what I mean?"

He stared at me for a long moment, his brown

eyes thoughtful. "Yeah, now that you mention it, I guess I do."

I was glad we were alone. I had waited until Wednesday, when I could get around pretty well with a cane, then I arranged to meet him at the library downtown, where I had to check out some books for a physics report. I wanted us to be in a place where Buddy would be too embarrassed to yell at me, even if he felt like it. So there we were, way at the back of the science section where no one ever goes anyway, holding this very quiet, very intense conversation.

"It's not that I don't like you," I was quick to put in. "Because I really do. I think you're a great person."

"Me, too. I mean, I think you're a great person, too. That's what I don't understand. If we're both such great people, how come we're breaking up?"

I sighed. "Sometimes there's no reason. It's just the way it is."

"Is there someone else?" The inevitable question. I should have known I wouldn't be able to avoid it.

"That's got nothing to do with it," I answered.

"You still haven't told me, though. Are you seeing some other guy?"

"No," I said. It was the truth.

I hadn't seen Richie since Saturday—except in social studies, which didn't really count since we barely spoke to each other there. I knew he was probably waiting for me to tell him I'd broken up with Buddy, but still it was hard just sitting there and staring at the back of his head for a whole period, not knowing what we would say to each other when we got the chance. Or if we would have anything to say at all.

"What about the prom?" Buddy asked. "Do you still want to go?"

I had completely forgotten about the prom. It was two weeks away—the same weekend as my mother's wedding, which seemed to overshadow everything in my life right then.

"You never asked me in the first place," I reminded him gently.

He shrugged. "I just figured you'd know."

"There. You see what I mean? About predictable?"

"Well—yeah, when you put it that way, I do. I guess I never thought about it that much before."

"That's how people get into ruts. You go along, taking things for granted, avoiding risks, then—boom, it hits you. All of a sudden something happens, and you realize how boring your life is."

Buddy was staring down at my foot, wrapped in its Ace bandage. "I think I understand," he said, nodding. Buddy is no dummy. "You and Richie, right? I guess I always knew it deep down. The way you two were always going at each other."

I could feel myself turning red. "I don't know what you mean."

"Look, I'm not going to blow up about it, if that's what you're worried about."

"I wasn't worried."

"Just don't ask me to congratulate you, either."

"Buddy." I touched his arm. "I meant what I said before. About the real reason for us breaking up. Do you believe me?"

He frowned. "Yeah, I guess I do. It's not so much whether or not I believe you. But I guess I felt it, too. Maybe not as much as you, or maybe I just didn't want to admit it to myself."

We stood there, looking at each other and feeling awkward now that everything had been said.

"Well, I should be getting home," I said, picking up the books I was going to check out and trying to juggle them with my cane.

Buddy watched me struggle for a minute, then with a sigh he scooped the books out of my hands. He glanced down at the titles and whistled. "Man, talk about boring!"

I smiled at him in relief. It looked like we could still be friends after all.

Later that night, I called Richie. My hands were sweating as I dialed his number. The phone rang five times before it was answered by a deep male voice.

"Richie? It's me, Joy." My heart was pounding so hard I could hardly hear myself talk.

"This isn't Richie," the voice said. "This is his brother Dan."

"Oh—sorry."

"Don't be—everybody says we sound alike."

"Is—is Richie there?"

"Naw—he's at basketball practice. I can give him a message, though, if you want. Who's this again?"

"Uh—Joy—Joy Wilder. Just tell him I called, OK?"

"Sure."

After I hung up, I saw that my hands were shaking. I decided I shouldn't have called. I should have waited until I saw Richie in school. Now I had no choice but to sit around chewing my nails while I waited for him to call me back. *If* he called me back.

In my opinion, waiting for the phone to ring is the worst kind of mental torture there is. You tell yourself you're not really expecting it to ring, but at the same time you're listening for it all the time, even while you're pretending to watch TV or do your homework. Hours go by and it doesn't ring. Then someone in your family, say your mother, goes in to use it, and you're sure the boy whose call you've been waiting for all night is now getting a busy signal. But, of course, you can't admit how anxious you are, so you sit there smiling while you want to strangle your own mother with the phone cord. Waiting for the phone to ring can drive you crazy.

I sat down to wait.

Chapter Thirteen

"Maybe he had a flat tire, and by the time he got home it was too late to call," Leona suggested without much conviction. "It happens sometimes, you know."

"Sure," I said. "In the movies."

"Well, maybe it didn't happen, but he still could have a good excuse anyway."

"Yeah, and I know what it is. He decided that what happened on the island was a case of temporary insanity."

That, at any rate, was the likeliest excuse I could come up with after spending an entire night waiting for Richie to call. Another possibility was that this whole thing was a big joke—at my expense. I half expected to find Richie perched on my desk the next time I walked into social studies, a huge grin plastered across his face. "Fooled you, didn't I?" he would say.

Needless to say, I was very depressed over the whole thing. It didn't help matters, either, that we were shopping for a dress for Leona to wear to the prom.

"What do you think of this one?" she asked, holding up a bright green off-the-shoulder formal made of some shimmery material.

"Too green," I said. "You'd look like a traffic light."

"You're right." Leona put it back and scanned the next rack. "Oh, look!" she said excitedly, taking down a long white dress with puffed sleeves and a pink sash.

"Perfect," I said. "If you were Little Bo Peep."

"Maybe I should save us the trouble of having to shop," she remarked dryly. "I could just wear my gorilla suit."

Leona is one of the few people you'll ever meet who actually owns a gorilla suit. I swear it's true. She saw it at a garage sale somewhere and couldn't resist buying it. It's ancient and has a very bad case of mange, along with a few missing teeth. She wore it last Halloween and managed to make a few people run from her, screaming.

Personally, I think it was more the smell that scared them than anything else.

"I can just see Sid trying to find a corsage that would go with a gorilla suit," I said.

Leona started cracking up at that one and couldn't stop. It got so bad, the saleslady began to give us these suspicious looks, like she wasn't quite sure what we were going to do next. Salesladies, I've found, are naturally suspicious of teenagers anyway, so it didn't help that we were behaving like a couple of escaped lunatics.

My ankle was starting to bother me, so we gave up looking at dresses for the time being and went over to the Polar Bear Shoppe for ice cream. Leona ordered a double butterscotch sundae with extra whipped cream and nuts. She's naturally skinny and has never had to diet in her life. It seems like I'm always dieting, and yet I'm never as thin as I want to be. Feeling semivirtuous, I ordered a single cone, and we went outside where they have these wrought-iron benches for the customers to sit on while they're eating.

"Do you know if Marcia Freeman is going to the prom?" I asked.

Leona wiped a blob of sauce from her chin. "Yeah, I think so. She sits next to me in trig, and

I heard her talking to somebody about it the other day."

"Did she say who she was going with?"

"I can't remember. Why the sudden interest in Marcia?"

"*I'm* not interested in her, but I think Richie might be."

"That's crazy. She's not even his type."

"What's so crazy about it? I'm not his type, either."

"Sure you are. You're both totally wacko."

"Thanks a lot."

"You're welcome. I really did mean it as a compliment. I happen to like crazy people. They're a lot more fun than normal ones." She scooped out a hole in her whipped cream and spooned some sauce into it. "Listen, Joy, I think you're making too much out of one unreturned phone call."

"Maybe so, but I still can't help being uptight about the whole thing. Do you realize it's been almost one whole week since Richie and I spoke to each other? Maybe I imagined that whole island bit. Maybe it never even happened."

"You haven't talked to him at all?" Leona had stopped eating and was staring at me in surprise.

I blushed. "Actually, I guess I've sort of been avoiding him myself up until now. I was afraid we wouldn't have anything to say to each other."

"What about social studies? Aren't you two in the same class?"

"I didn't go today. I couldn't stand the idea of facing him after waiting all of last night for him to phone, so I chickened out and cut class."

"Ah." Leona wiggled her spoon overhead. "The plot thickens. While Richie is ignoring you, you're busy running away from him. Sounds like the beginning of a great romance."

"Leona, be serious, will you? I really don't know what to do." I sighed. "Sometimes I really wish I still hated Richie. Things were a lot easier when I did. At least then I knew where I stood."

"Which was exactly nowhere. Seriously, Joy, I think you should talk to him. Running away isn't going to solve anything."

"I can't."

"Why not?"

"Because. Just because. I wouldn't know what to say."

"How about 'Hi, Richie,' for openers."

"Very funny. You know what I mean. What comes after that? 'Hi, Richie, I just wanted to say it was great kissing you back when we were

107

marooned on that island, and by the way, thanks for saving my life'?"

"Not bad."

"Leona!"

"OK, I was only kidding." She licked the last of the whipped cream from her spoon. "I can't tell you exactly what you should say, but all I know is that the longer you wait, the bigger this whole thing is going to seem. What about the prom? You want him to ask you to that, don't you?"

"But what if he doesn't want to go with me? He's probably taking Marcia."

"That's positive thinking for you," she said. "Come on, Joy, it can't be as bad as all that. What about your mother's wedding? Didn't you say he was invited to that?"

"Yeah, but I doubt if he'll come."

Even while I was saying it, I hoped he would come. I had already dreamed up this fantasy where he came to the wedding, and no words of explanation were necessary—we just fell into each other's arms.

I also had this other fantasy where my mom was marrying someone her own age. Someone who would be content to sit around reading the paper and smoking a pipe while our lives carried on as usual around him.

Real life isn't like that, I know. In real life, boys you think like you don't call, and mothers get married to men with saws and hammers instead of pipes.

Maybe I was just kidding myself, I thought. Maybe it all did happen, but not the way I remembered it. Maybe I was stretching the facts, the way you do when you describe something nice that happened to you and you want to make it sound even nicer, so you exaggerate a little. You make it a B+ instead of a plain old B. Or you say he kissed you on the lips when he really only kissed your cheek and got a corner of your mouth by mistake.

Maybe I had just talked myself into believing Richie was falling in love with me when he was really just being nice for a change.

I'd been lost in these thoughts for quite a while; so I was startled when Leona nudged me. "I don't get it," she said. "You're always telling us not to give up, no matter what. How come you're not taking your own advice?"

I looked at her and sighed. "Nobody takes their own advice. If everybody did, there'd be no one left to give it to."

"You always have a very definite, strong way of looking at things, Joy," observed Leona. "I guess that's why you have such a fatal attraction for Richie."

"Fatal is right. I think whatever attraction there was is probably dead. On his part, that is." I got up and tossed my crumpled napkin into the nearest trash can. "Come on, let's see if we can find something that will top your gorilla suit."

I didn't really feel like doing any more shopping, but I wasn't about to let my mood ruin the day for Leona. The way it works with best friends is that when you're really miserable, your friend usually can't have a good time without feeling guilty. I knew Leona felt guilty enough about going to the prom when I wasn't, so I didn't want to make it any worse.

As far as I was concerned, though, things couldn't have been worse.

Chapter Fourteen

I was late walking into social studies the next day, and Richie was already sitting in his usual place—slouched down in his chair, with his eyes fixed on the movie Mr. Jaeger was showing. The movie was about race riots in the South as far as I could see—something to do with the special study we were doing on prejudice. There were a lot of people running around screaming at one another and throwing bottles and things. It fit my mood at the moment.

I slid into my seat, trying hard not to look at Richie. I was sure the whole class could hear my heart thundering. Throughout the movie, my eyes kept straying over to him. There was something utterly fascinating about the way the light from the projector shone through the top of his hair, outlining each individual curl. He was turned sort of sideways in his chair, with one elbow hooked over the back. I concentrated on his forearm, the way the muscles bulged up and the hair grew light and downy, a contrast to the hair on his head.

When the movie ended, there was a short question-and-answer period.

"When we think of prejudice, we most often think of color barriers," Mr. Jaeger was saying. "But what about other kinds of prejudice? The kinds we don't always recognize ourselves? Can anyone give me an example of what I'm talking about?"

A plump arm shot up.

"Fat," said Jennalee Kingsley. "Most people are very prejudiced against fat. Like if you're fat and you go into a store, they always wait on you last. Then half the time they treat you like you're retarded or something."

Jennalee weighs about two hundred pounds but never seems embarrassed about it. She wears bright clothes and lots of jewelry. Once when the snack machine in the cafeteria broke down and they were giving away ice-cream sandwiches that would've melted otherwise, I watched Jennalee help herself to four, right on the spot, without batting an eyelash.

"Being short is no picnic, either," put in Bill Sanchez. "I once asked a girl out, and she told me she only dated guys who were at least two inches taller than she was."

"What does she do—get her ruler out before every date?" someone in the back asked, prompting a storm of snickers.

"I think age is one of the worst kinds of discrimination," said Bridgett Thompson, a slim, redheaded girl who sat in front of me. "When you're a kid, nobody ever listens to you or takes you seriously. I mean, it's like your opinions don't count if you're under thirty."

"I'm listening," countered Mr. Jaeger with a smile, but we all knew a teacher who wore denim jackets and Frye boots to school was the exception to the grown-up rule.

John Henley, a tall, black-haired boy, raised his hand. "Bridgett is right. What I think is really unfair, though, is how it's OK for a girl to go out with someone who's a couple of years older than her, but just let a guy try the same thing. A girl who was older than him would probably die laughing if he asked her out."

I thought about Paul and how prejudiced I'd been about his age. I remembered all the times

I'd accused Richie of being a male chauvinist. Well, maybe I'd been an age chauvinist.

Our homework assignment for the weekend was to write an essay about our own particular prejudice. Lost in thought, I didn't notice until it was too late that I'd fallen into step with Richie as I was leaving class.

We looked at each other, then, embarrassed, our glances slid down to the floor. I had a burning desire to run away at that moment, but it was too late. I licked my lips, opened my mouth to say something, but my voice emerged as a croak.

"How's it going?" Richie asked. His eyes were darting all over the hallway, looking at everything but me.

"Fine," I said. Brilliant.

"What did you think of the movie?"

"It was OK. Pretty violent, though."

"Yeah, well, I guess that was the whole point."

The old Richie would've said something like, "Can't take it, huh, J.W.?" Then I probably would have gotten mad and told him to take a long walk off a short pier. But I didn't know how to talk to this strange new Richie who stood before me now, looking as uncomfortable and embarrassed as I felt.

In spite of everything, I lingered, hoping he might mention something about what had passed between us on the island.

Richie cleared his throat. "How's your foot?"

"Better. This is the first day I haven't had to use a cane." I swallowed hard. "Richie—I, uh—I wanted to thank you for—well, everything you did."

He blushed. "Forget it. It was nothing."

Nothing. The word echoed in my mind. What did he mean by it? Nothing, as in unimportant, inconsequential, forgettable? Did *I* mean nothing as well?

I wanted to tell him about Buddy, but the words stuck in my throat. After all, he hadn't even bothered to call me back the other night. Would it matter to him that Buddy and I had broken up? Maybe he already knew and didn't care.

Richie glanced up at the clock overhead. "We probably should get going if we want to make our next classes on time. What do you have next?"

"PE, believe it or not. I can't run or do anything, but I have to show up, anyway."

"I've got to get my homework out of my locker

115

before I go to English. Can I help you with your books or something?"

I shook my head. He didn't really want to carry my books. It was obvious he was only being polite. "No, thanks, I can manage. I'm really fine."

"Oh—Well, OK, then." For a second he stared at me, and I thought he looked disappointed. Then he was dashing off, tossing a hasty "See ya!" over his shoulder.

He hadn't said anything about my phone call. He hadn't mentioned one word about the prom.

My throat was so tight, I was sure I was going to burst into tears any second. I could feel my cheeks burning, and there was an uncomfortable throbbing in my chest. Richie had made it all too plain how he felt about me now. Or, rather, how he *didn't* feel. Now I was angry as well as miserable. How dare he treat me this way? I had made a fool of myself over him, and now he was ignoring me.

I was ducking into the bathroom, thankful that at least I hadn't run into anyone I knew, when a blinding light flashed in front of me.

"Smile—you're on 'Candid Camera'!" chirped Sandy.

He scuttled off quickly before I could break his camera over his head.

Chapter Fifteen

I spent the following Friday night—the night of the prom—alone, watching *The African Queen* on TV. It's one of my favorite old movies, but that time I could hardly stand to watch it. It reminded me too much of Richie. It's about this man and this missionary lady who can't stand each other at first, then they get stuck on a boat together somewhere in the wilds of Africa. After shooting a few rapids and having a few other hairy experiences, they start getting to like each other, and by the end of the movie, they're madly in love and get married. Of course, there's much more to it than that, but that's the gist of it—how two people who don't seem to have any-thing in common can fall in love anyway.

No one else was home, so I was free to wallow in my misery. I cried my way through the last half of the movie, thinking about Richie and how he was probably at the prom having a great time with Marcia Freeman. I could just picture them, sailing around the dance floor while they gazed longingly into each other's eyes. "Richie, I heard you were stuck on an island all day with Joy Wilder," she would whisper in his ear. "Oh, it was nothing," he would answer.

I got so depressed about the whole situation that I ended up eating my way through an entire quart of chocolate swirl ice cream. Afterward I really felt sick. I cried some more, then went upstairs and crawled into bed, not even bothering to take off my jeans and sweatshirt. When I closed my eyes, all I could see was Richie kissing me, gently the first time, then more passionately. . . .

Why was I torturing myself this way? It was obvious he didn't care about me. Why should I care about him?

A couple of months before, I'd read this book about self-hypnosis. Supposedly, if you learned how to hypnotize yourself, you could accomplish all kinds of things you never thought you could have done otherwise. There was a man who hypnotized himself into making a million dollars. Another one cured himself of chronic arthritis. I wondered if it was possible for me to cure myself of Richie the same way.

"I hate Richie Brennan," I muttered to myself while lying there, staring up at the ceiling. "He means nothing to me, absolutely nothing." Tears were sliding down my temples into my hair. "I don't care if I never see him again. I don't care if he's having a terrific time at the prom with Marcia. I don't care if he's got sexy blue eyes and a fantastic body. . . ."

Chapter Sixteen

Saturday morning while everyone else was running around like crazy getting ready for the wedding, I drove down to the bus station to pick up Grandpa.

"What is this—no Rolls-Royce?" Grandpa asked teasingly when he saw the Pontiac parked by the curb. "I was hoping I could show up for this wedding in style."

"Sorry, Grandpa, but Mom wants to play this low-key. She doesn't want anyone to know we're millionaires."

Seeing Grandpa was the first good thing about that weekend. I threw my arms around him and hugged him close. "Gee, it's great to be with you," I said happily.

"It's even better to be with you," Grandpa answered, giving me a kiss on the head. "So, how's the bride holding up?" he asked. "She must be getting pretty jumpy about now."

"She's fine. Yesterday she wasn't too happy about the way they did her hair, but she's feeling OK about it now."

In the old days when my mother found a gray hair, she'd just laugh and ignore it, but ever since she met Paul she'd been putting rinses on her hair regularly.

"Actually," I went on as I loaded his suitcase into the trunk, "Paul's the one to worry about. He says he faints easily. I just hope he doesn't pass out at the altar. He'd probably crush Mom."

Grandpa slung an arm around my shoulders. "Think we might be able to hold him up? Between the two of us?"

"Sure thing, Grandpa."

When we got back to the house, Mom was turning her room upside down looking for a missing shoe. Wearing the other one, she limped over to kiss Grandpa's cheek.

"Hi, Dad! Sorry everything is such a madhouse. Do you believe this? Paul and Kev left early so they could put the roses over the bower. Oh, I almost forgot!" She bumped the heel of her hand against her forehead. "I was supposed to phone Mrs. Klein and remind her to pick up the cake. The bakery called yesterday, and their delivery van is—" She broke off as she spotted her shoe peeping out from under the bed. She put it on, then sat down and started to laugh. Then all of a sudden she wasn't laughing anymore. She was crying.

Grandpa looked at Mom and then at me. It was obvious that he thought she and I should have a woman-to-woman talk. "How about a soda anybody? I could sure use one myself."

Subtle.

"In the fridge, Grandpa. Bottom shelf."

When Grandpa had left, I sat down next to Mom and put my arm around her. It felt funny to be the one consoling her instead of having it the other way around, especially since I didn't know what I was consoling her about. Mom didn't seem to know, either.

"I don't know why I'm crying," she said, sniffing. "It's ridiculous. I spent an hour putting on my makeup and now look at me."

"You look great," I told her. "Fantastic. Paul's going to flip when he sees you."

She managed a watery smile. "You really think so?" she asked, as if he hadn't seen her a million times already.

Besides, it was true. I'd always thought it was

a cliché, that stuff about blushing brides and all, but that day my mother really did look prettier than usual. Special. She was wearing this pale sky-blue dress with long, billowy sleeves. Her hair was done up in a kind of loose crown with tiny rosebuds and sprigs of baby's breath tucked in around the edges. She looked about my age.

"Paul's really lucky," I said, thinking out loud.

"I'm lucky, too," she said. "You know something, Joy? A long time ago I used to think that when two people got married, everything had to be just right between the two of them. Like packages on a shelf. You know, lined up according to size, shape, and color."

"And age?"

She squeezed my hand. "Yeah, that too. But it's not true. You don't find love. It finds you. And it's hardly ever what you'd expect."

I nodded slowly, thinking about Richie and me. "I think I know what you mean."

Mom dried her eyes with a tissue. When she looked up, she was smiling hopefully. "Joy, I'm not asking you to love Paul as much as I do. Just give him a chance. OK?"

"I'll try."

"I know you will, honey. And I know it isn't

easy for you." She glanced at the clock. "Oh, gosh, we have to be there in twenty minutes!"

"I hope I can find *my* shoes," I said, laughing. "And get dressed *and* get us there on time."

Mom leaned over and kissed me on the cheek. "Thanks," she said.

"For what?" I asked.

"For being Joy Wilder, that's what."

I wasn't sure exactly what that meant, but I thought I understood sort of what Mom was trying to say. She was telling me I didn't have to try to be somebody I wasn't—I just had to try to be the best *I* could be.

The wedding turned out to be really nice, unlike some weddings I'd been to in my time. I once went to this wedding where the bandleader at the reception made all the kids come up to the dance floor, and then he divided us up into two groups—the Coke team and the Pepsi team. If you were on the Coke team, you had to dance with someone on the Pepsi team. I was really embarrassed the whole time because this ten-year-old kid on the other team kept picking me. I was fourteen then, and he only came up to my shoulder. Cute, huh?

At Mom and Paul's wedding, there was only a guitarist who sat on a chair under the trees and played quietly, mostly classical stuff. Everything went pretty smoothly, except when my aunt Roberta bumped into a rosebush and tore a big hole in the back of her dress. Then one of my little cousins turned on the sprinklers by mistake, and a few people got slightly wet. But everybody had had a few glasses of champagne by then, so nobody got mad.

I went up to Paul after the ceremony when the food was being set out on long tables in the shade. "I'm glad you didn't faint."

"Yeah, so am I. It was a close call, though. I was pretty nervous." He was looking over at Mom, and he had this big, sappy grin on his face, but for once I didn't mind.

"It was nice," I said. "I liked the part where you read that poem to Mom."

"Tennyson."

"I didn't know you liked poetry."

He turned his grin on me. "Yeah, well—I'm a jack of many trades besides carpentry. I'll have to show you my arrowhead collection sometime. I used to collect them when I was a kid."

"I don't believe you were ever a kid."

"Sure I was. In fact, I was the only six-foot ten-year-old on our block. My mother used to pack cigars in my lunch box because she heard somewhere that they stunt your growth."

"You're making that up!" I laughed.

Paul put his hand on my shoulder and said, "You're OK, kid." Then he disappeared into the crowd again. The next time I saw him, he and my mother were standing by this big lilac bush, holding hands and gazing at each other as if no one else existed. I wouldn't have minded it at all if it hadn't reminded me of Richie. Every time I thought about him I got this tight feeling in my chest.

Kevin ran up to me just as Paul and Mom were getting ready to cut the cake. "Mom says I can have as much cake as I want. But I have to wait for seconds until everybody's had a piece."

"Just don't get sick on the way home," I told him.

"Don't worry. I'll stick my head out the window." As we watched Mom cram a piece of cake into Paul's mouth, I felt a small, moist hand creep into mine. "Joy? Are you glad he's really our stepfather now?"

I thought about it for a moment, then answered truthfully, "Sure I'm glad."

Kevin seemed satisfied with that, and a minute later he was attacking the cake like a starved animal. I wasn't too hungry myself, so I got a paper cup of 7-Up and found a dry spot on the grass to sit on.

All this time I'd been trying hard not to think about Richie. Part of me had been wildly hoping that he would show up, even though I knew how unlikely that was. Why couldn't I just forget about him the same way he'd forgotten about me?

After the cake had been polished off, the crowd started thinning out, and the newlyweds decided it was time to go. Paul's van was already loaded up with the camping gear the two of them would need for their honeymoon, so all they had to do was change into their regular clothes and take off. Mom hugged us both and told Kevin to behave for Grandpa while she was gone. Then she tossed her bouquet, only she had to do it twice. The first time it got stuck on a tree branch. The second time, my cousin Lucy caught it.

I suppose I could have caught it myself if I'd tried, but at the crucial moment something distracted my attention. I caught sight of a familiar face peering out of the crowd. My heart started to pound. When had Richie arrived?

He spotted me and waved. I tried to wave back, but my arm wouldn't move. I could only stand there like a mummy while Richie walked over to where I was standing.

Chapter Seventeen

"Hi," he said.

"You're late," I told him. "They already cut the cake."

"I didn't come for the cake."

He was wearing dark slacks and a pastel blue shirt that matched his eyes. His hair curlicued in damp ringlets as if he'd just gotten out of the shower.

"What did you come for then?" I asked.

"I wanted to talk to you."

"OK. I'm listening," I said flatly. "What did you want to talk about?"

"Not here. Can we go for a walk or something?"

I looked around. Most of the guests were getting ready to leave anyway, except Lucy, who was still squealing over the bouquet. The caterering crew had begun clearing away what was left of the food.

I shrugged. "I guess it's OK. Just let me tell Grandpa first." I was back in a minute, and we left.

We walked a couple of blocks before he spoke.

"I heard you broke up with Buddy," he said. He was frowning. "Why didn't you tell me?"

I shrugged again. "I didn't think you'd be interested."

"I see." He kicked at a leaf that was on the sidewalk. "You figured I wouldn't care one way or the other, is that right?"

"Something like that."

"I don't understand," he said.

"What?"

"You!"

Richie stopped in the middle of the sidewalk and threw his hands up. His eyes blazed with anger. "Here I am, practically a nervous wreck from wondering if you were really going to break up with Buddy—and wondering if you'd forgotten that day we spent on the island—and you act like it was nothing. Like it was all a big joke or something. I should have known, the way you were acting the other day—"

"The way *I* was acting!" I stared at him in disbelief. "*You* were the one who acted like *you* didn't care!"

"Me? I was waiting for you to say something. When you didn't, I just assumed you'd changed your mind about us."

"I called you. How come you didn't call me back?"

"You called me?" Now it was his turn to look surprised.

"I talked to your brother. He said he'd tell you."

Suddenly Richie started to laugh. "My brother Dan has a memory the size of a pea. He never remembers anything."

"You mean you never got my message?"

"Is that all that's been bothering you? Is it because I didn't call you back?"

"Well—sort of. To be honest, I guess I was just as worried as you were," I admitted. "I couldn't be sure how you felt. On the island . . . the way it was—like—like make-believe. . . . I didn't know if you'd feel the same way once we got back to reality."

"You should have talked to me," Richie said, exasperated.

"I was waiting for you to talk to me!"

"OK, I get the message. You don't have to yell."

"Who's yelling?"

132

"You are!"

Now we were both yelling. A few people walking by or out mowing their lawns stopped to stare at us. A family in a green station wagon slowed down as it passed us. A couple of kids in the backseat were leaning out the window with bug-eyed expressions.

We glared at each other for a minute, then we both started to laugh.

"Are you mad?" Richie asked.

I shook my head. "No. I was, but I'm not anymore."

"Good."

Without warning, Richie drew me to him and kissed me, right there out in the open in front of the whole world. But I forgot we weren't alone the instant his lips touched mine. If love has a taste, that's what Richie's kiss tasted like. Sweet and tingly, like the champagne I'd sipped at the wedding. I felt myself start to melt from the neck down. It was a slow, sliding, warm feeling. There was a fluttering inside me, as if a butterfly were trapped there, beating its wings against my rib cage trying to get out. Richie's arms tightened around me as our kiss deepened. A drumming sound filled my ears.

Then I realized it was the sound of someone

clapping. I pulled away and looked around. A young bearded man who had been trimming his hedge across the street was applauding us. My cheeks flamed with embarrassment, but I'd never been so happy in my whole life.

"What do we do for an encore?" I whispered to Richie.

"I don't know. We'll think of something."

I slipped my hand into his, and we started walking again. After a minute or two Richie said, "You're something else, you know that, J.W.?"

"You, too, R.B."

He looked over at me and grinned.

"Do you think we'll be able to get along now that we're not fighting anymore?" he asked.

I smiled. "Shut up and kiss me, creep, and let's give it a try."

SWEET DREAMS are fresh, fun and exciting,—alive with the flavor of the contemporary teen scene—the joy and doubt of *first love*. If you've missed any SWEET DREAMS titles, from #1 to #100, then you're missing out on *your* kind of stories, written about people like *you*!

☐	24837	**DAY DREAMER #32** Janet Quin-Harkin	**$2.25**
☐	24336	**FORBIDDEN LOVE #35** Marian Woodruff	**$2.25**
☐	24338	**SUMMER DREAMS #36** Barbara Conklin	**$2.25**
☐	24340	**FIRST LOVE #39** Debra Spector	**$2.25**
☐	24838	**THE TRUTH ABOUT ME AND BOBBY V. #41** Janetta Johns	**$2.25**
☐	24341	**DREAM PROM #45** Margaret Burman	**$2.25**
☐	24688	**SECRET ADMIRER #81** Debra Spector	**$2.25**
☐	24383	**HEY, GOOD LOOKING #82** Jane Polcovar	**$2.25**
☐	24823	**LOVE BY THE BOOK #83** Anne Park	**$2.25**
☐	24718	**THE LAST WORD #84** Susan Blake	**$2.25**
☐	24890	**THE BOY SHE LEFT BEHIND #85** Suzanne Rand	**$2.25**
☐	24945	**QUESTIONS OF LOVE #86** Rosemary Vernon	**$2.25**
☐	24824	**PROGRAMMED FOR LOVE #87** Marion Crane	**$2.25**
☐	24891	**WRONG KIND OF BOY #88** Shannon Blair	**$2.25**
☐	24946	**101 WAYS TO MEET MR. RIGHT #89** Janet Quin-Harkin	**$2.25**
☐	24992	**TWO'S A CROWD #90** Diana Gregory	**$2.25**
☐	25070	**THE LOVE HUNT #91** Yvonne Green	**$2.25**
☐	25131	**KISS & TELL #92** Janet Quin-Harkin	**$2.25**
☐	25071	**THE GREAT BOY CHASE #93** Janet Quin-Harkin	**$2.25**
☐	25132	**SECOND CHANCES #94** Nancy Levinso	**$2.25**
☐	25178	**NO STRINGS ATTACHED #95** Eileen Hehl	**$2.25**
☐	25179	**FIRST, LAST, AND ALWAYS #96** Barbara Conklin	**$2.25**

Prices and availability subject to change without notice.

SWEET VALLEY HIGH

☑	25143	**POWER PLAY #4**	$2.50
☐	25043	**ALL NIGHT LONG #5**	$2.50
☐	25105	**DANGEROUS LOVE #6**	$2.50
☐	25106	**DEAR SISTER #7**	$2.50
☐	25092	**HEARTBREAKER #8**	$2.50
☐	25026	**RACING HEARTS #9**	$2.50
☐	25016	**WRONG KIND OF GIRL #10**	$2.50
☐	25046	**TOO GOOD TO BE TRUE #11**	$2.50
☐	25035	**WHEN LOVE DIES #12**	$2.50
☐	24524	**KIDNAPPED #13**	$2.25
☐	24531	**DECEPTIONS #14**	$2.50
☐	24582	**PROMISES #15**	$2.50
☐	24672	**RAGS TO RICHES #16**	$2.50
☐	24723	**LOVE LETTERS #17**	$2.50
☐	24825	**HEAD OVER HEELS #18**	$2.50
☐	24893	**SHOWDOWN #19**	$2.50
☐	24947	**CRASH LANDING! #20**	$2.50

Prices and availability subject to change without notice.

Buy them at your local bookstore or use this handy coupon for ordering:

Bantam Books, Inc., Dept SVH, 414 East Golf Road, Des Plaines, Ill. 60016

Please send me the books I have checked above. I am enclosing $_____
(please add $1.50 to cover postage and handling). Send check or money order
—no cash or C.O.D.'s please.

Mr/Mrs/Miss _____

Address_____

City_____ State/Zip_____

SVH—1/86

Please allow four to six weeks for delivery. This offer expires 7/86.

Special Offer
Buy a Bantam Book
for only 50¢.

Now you can order the exciting books you've been wanting to read straight from Bantam's latest listing of hundreds of titles. *And* this special offer gives you the opportunity to purchase a Bantam book for only 50¢. Here's how:

By ordering any five books at the regular price per order, you can also choose any other single book listed (up to $4.95 value) for only 50¢. Some restrictions do apply, so for further details send for Bantam's listing of titles today.

Just send us your name and address and we'll send you Bantam Book's SHOP AT HOME CATALOG!